Night Butterflies

A Tony Ford Crime Novel
Copyright 2017
ISBN: 978-0-9958169-2-3

Published in Canada

Also by Larry Flewin

The Pavilion

The 26th Letter

CHAPTER ONE

My left eyeball swirled around like a lazy aggie, trying to figure out where the hell I was and why everything hurt so much. It finally focused on the dust on the floor. I recognised that dust, it was mine, because those were my good shoes sitting in the middle of it. Last time I'd seen them they were under my desk. That meant I was home and safe but it wasn't my bed I was lying on. I didn't have one.

Gradually, a couple of cylinders began to fire and I slowly got up onto my knees, shaking out the cobwebs and getting the jaw working. My left arm hurt like hell. I tried to brush away the pain but my fingers came back red and sticky. Something bad must have happened last night but I couldn't remember what. Seems I couldn't go anywhere without somebody somewhere taking an exception to my presence.

Standing took a little longer and I made it only as far as my desk before collapsing on top of it like a stiff on a slab. It wasn't much more comfortable than the floor but at least I wasn't sucking up any more dust. Took a few deep breaths, heaved myself to my feet again and staggered over to the sink. The mirror wasn't any friendlier.

So, that's what the floor looked like. It was plastered all over the right side of my face, neck and shirt. And it didn't taste any better than it looked. Cranked open a pair of squeaky taps, filled the sink with the rusty brown crud that passed for water in this part of town and threw it all over myself. The crease on my arm cried out in pain with the effort. No idea where it had come from but it matched the older one farther up my arm.

I wasn't in the habit of collecting bodily abrasions but in mine of work you can't avoid them. I was just hoping the other guy had a bigger hole. Tugged the remains of my liquid dinner out of my hip pocket, poured some of it over my arm, and wrapped it up tight with a hankie. The rest I downed in one long pull, for medicinal purposes. I only had the one shirt so the hole and the pink stain stayed.

Found a half pack of Lucky Strikes in my jacket along with a heavy Zippo lighter. Steel case, good quality engraving, nice blue flame with the first flick. Not mine but I knew the owner. He wasn't going to be asking for it back any time soon. It took both hands to light a smoke and get it to my lips, like fire going in but smooth and cool blowing out. A couple of deep draws and a fit of coughing and I was awake as I was going to get. And that was breakfast.

The sun was already well up in the sky, a welcome sight most days, but in my condition like staring into a searchlight. I squinted hard, drying off in the sun while scratching a peephole in the dust on my window. I was curious to know what day it was, what time it might be, all those good things. Didn't have my watch to hand, it was in hock along with some other stuff I'd collected over the years. Not trophies exactly but little reminders of who, what, and when. There was a story came with each one, some of them too strange to tell.

The paint on the door said Tony Ford, Private Investigations, the swirling gold letters chipped in places and faded by time. Guy I knew, ex-parolee, had lettered the door for me. A snappy new look for my office and suddenly my bad memory couldn't place him anywhere near a mugging he was up for. That was more than a few years ago. At the time, I was still young enough, and dumb enough, to think I could take on the whole world and clean up all the crap it woke up to every morning. Not anymore.

Home and office was a single large room with a sink and a closet, second floor front of a two-storey walk up. I shared the facilities down the hall but they didn't get much use. Everything I owned or cared about fit in my pockets. And all my desk did was hold down the floor and the telephone. It didn't ring much and to tell the truth, I didn't always answer it. Word of mouth was what kept me going, kept me alive.

The one door opened in towards the desk, giving me of couple seconds in case I didn't like who was calling. A large, brown leather lump of chair sat in the dark in the corner, as creased and as worn out as its owner. Did a lot of thinking and drinking in it, slept in it a lot, gave me something to kick when things went south. Like I said, not a big place.

Me, I'm a shoe leather PI. You ain't dead until I can't feel a pulse and the case ain't closed until I hear the crackle of cash in my pocket. No paperwork, no receipts, no secretary, just me and my .45

calibre friend. Got back from the big one alive, said hello to life and living for a coupla years, then picked up this racket when the money and the good times ran out. Business was good at first, so much so I almost took on a partner. But he got himself killed working a stakeout with me. I was watching her instead of watching out for him.

Decided to go it alone after that and did pretty good for a while. Nothing really big, just a lot of small stuff, divorces and the like, and the odd missing person or runaway accountant. Seemed life was too good for a lot of people and mistakes were made, bad ones. Which is where I came in. I did what needed doing and didn't ask a lot of questions. For the most part business was okay but I wasn't going to get rich, and not a lot of thanks came my way.

So, how many years later I looked and felt much the same as the lettering on the door, suggesting a less than ideal career choice.

Life had gotten a whole lot harder. The papers said these were the dog days of summer, but the two-legged kind had long since run out of money and luck. Dark times had replaced the easy living of only a few years ago. There used to be long line-ups for theatres and clubs but now the lines were just as long for food, work, and a place to sleep for the night. Didn't matter where you went, or who you were, it was always the same, back of the line buddy, and best of luck to you. Mine had been holding up pretty well to this point but work had started to thin out a little. Maybe it was the price of lead.

I've learned to appreciate that there's always a story behind the story and that it's never very pretty. People pay me to find that out, but unlike those public servants who wear a badge and draw a steady paycheque, I take cash for my services. Cheques rely on good faith, cash doesn't. I've been paid in meals, dressed in a new suit and shoes, and just plain told to go to hell. One guy even sent over his wife for an evening of recreation, but I passed. Even I know when to draw the line.

And that's what had missing for the last while, cash, or it's reasonable facsimile. Out on the street and hard at it is what I'm good at. A slow day on the job is agony, which explains the pain I've been in for the last few weeks. All I'd been able to accomplish lately was to stare out the window and watch life's parade.

My last real case had paid out just over three weeks ago, courtesy of some schmuck who tabbed me while I was downstairs checking for mail that wasn't there. Some weedy little nothing with beady eyes, a pencil moustache and a bowtie wanted someone followed and didn't want the whole world to know. Just come see me at my office, give me a quick update and I'll pay you cash for your time. Plus expenses, I added. Whatever, just find out what's going on. Here's her picture, she's usually at this address, just see where she goes and what she does.

As it turned out I was following the missus who was following him while he chased some skirt around a hotel room. Didn't know who the office help was, but at a guess she was his secretary, as good at taking her clothes off as she was at dictation. The shadow that had him worried, the one waking him up in a cold sweat at night, turned out to be as good a hunter as I was.

We got to the same hotel room door at the same time. She was packing, same as me. Gotta love a brunette with a temper. Ever the gentleman, I held the door open for her while she charged in and raised six kinds of hell. Don't know what the final outcome was but I got cash from him and a very bad memory of her. Another day on the job.

All of which didn't amount to a hill of beans if people weren't doing bad things to each other. I didn't think it was possible but it sure seemed that way for a while. Nothing crossed my desk other than starving flies and final demands. It was like the town had sobered up and gone on the straight and narrow. Nobody was playing with guns or knives, leaving me nothing else to do but clean my gun and polish my ammunition. Hurry up and wait, just like the old days.

My only other play to stay in the game was to do just that, play. Poker. Five card stud one three-card draw no limit, a man's game. The kind of amusement that needed only a small room, a couple of chairs and a table, and a whole lot of other people's money to make it the best game in town. Throw in a good stogie and a decent scotch and I was in until the cows came home.

I was the house shill, the seat-man. All I had to do was show up, keep my iron out of sight, and make sure the neighbours didn't complain. A cash only gig courtesy of a good ol' girl named Stella. She would front me some spreading around money, all of which I gave back; I kept five percent of whatever the house made. Her associates and I would play until our arms ached and our wallets were empty, generally all night. And what better way to pass the time on a warm prairie night than bluff your way through two pair.

This was one of a number of lucrative side lines of my benefactress, Stella "Five Star" Johnson. She ran the greasy spoon I frequented, mainly because she fried everything that moved, and let me run a tab. A great big fat old world momma was Stella, with a lot of stuff on the go, and a lot of names at her fingertips.

We weren't all that close but we did play off of each other a lot. She yelled at the cook, I ate, and in between courses we spat out bits and pieces of this and that, the kind of things that could save a life or get one shot up real bad.

Real estate was dirt cheap what with businesses dropping like flies. For Sale signs were everywhere but she seemed to be the only one with cash. Always on the phone by the kitchen door yapping to somebody about this heap or that. Buy one here sell one there, god knows to whom, but she always came up golden on the deal. Brought a smile to those chubby little cheeks of hers that was downright scary. She had more faith in the future than most of us had in the present but then who was I to argue. My present came with a knife and fork and an empty plate.

Rooms to let were a dime a dozen, and with no renters around she'd toss me the keys and send a few friends my way. Poker, it seemed, was the one constant in this burned-out burg. Despite the dark times, the lines for bread and soup, and the desperation that passed for life for so many, everyone wanted in on the action. A man could be down to his last dime and he'd ante up just to get in on that one last hand. Like a drunk with the shakes it was the next hand that was going to change everything, and when it didn't it would be the one after that.

Typically, I'd set up shop in a second or third floor suite somewhere, stock it with cheap liquor and smokes and throw some chairs around a table. There was always a deli open somewhere so

I'd whistle up a couple of plates of chew long towards midnight. It was better than being shot at and I got home standing up, though not always sober. A bonus for me.

We were six tonight, sitting around the kitchen table of an empty apartment on the second floor of a tired, three-storey, walk-up. There were Scotch, Bourbon, and beer bottles everywhere, all open and mostly empty. The flies ignored them to buzz around the plates of half-eaten corned beef sandwiches and pickles heaped up on the counter behind us.

My compadres this particular evening were a lively bunch, half corked from all the booze we'd been inhaling, and bleary-eyed from all the smoke we had been exhaling. All of them except for the Fan, a weaselly, pin-striped suit, with slicked back hair and a bent pinkie. He'd done nothing more than play like a girl all night and lose his shirt, fanning himself with his cards every time chance didn't go his way. When he passed out at about two am, we stopped just long enough to drag him over to the sofa and empty his wallet into the pot.

Two of the other players, Mungo and Parker, I knew. These two lamebrains were paper pushers from over at City Hall with nothing but time on their hands and fat government paycheques in their pockets. They licensed cats, dogs, cars, and bicycles, and when no one was looking, wrote up nice new permits for .45s and .38s. They were frequent guests and had government-issue hands, pink and smooth and well-manicured.

The Cowboy sitting across from me was a new player. Stella sent players like him over once in a while, to lighten the mood and fatten the pot. Didn't say where he was from and I didn't ask but his clothes and his lingo said ex-con. His money was good and so were his instincts, judging by the fact that most of the night's winnings sat in front of him. His hands were sandpaper rough, smoking fingers stained a deep yellow from long habit. He had come along with the Fatman and the Fan, two more of Stella's semi-usuals.

Mortician was the gig claimed by the Fatman, but I couldn't figure how someone that big could even breath let alone heave bodies around all day. He smiled a stupid smile at that comment and proceeded to toss a handful of wedding rings into the pot. Gold he wheezed, jingling his pocket with a pudgy hand, eighteen carat and still warm. Charming.

The cards were worn thin and greasy to the touch. Crappy little hunks of paper that flew across the table like the lame ducks they were. It took a practised hand to get them to the players, and not into the pool of stale beer surrounding the pot. That was the hand to watch because it told a story every time. Who the winner was, who the loser was, and who the cheat was. As a kid I remember reading westerns, how the lawman could look into a gunslinger's eyes and figure his next move. I learned the hard way that it wasn't the eye that pulled a trigger or broke a nose or thumbed an ace.

It was long towards dawn and everything we owned was on the table. This was the last round and we were all in regardless. The hands dealing these little beauties belonged to me. Browned by the sun and creased with age, they shuffled and dealt with practised ease. All night long I had seen any number of good hands come and go but my mind just wasn't in it. Just one of those nights I guess, drunk as hell and hurtin' for cash, but just couldn't catch a break.

I shuffled my hand mindlessly before fanning it open and getting the surprise of my life. I had a full house, aces over eights! Not too shabby considering how the rest of the evening had progressed. That I had a full house was enough to wake me up and move my heart up a little closer to my throat. My last chance for a big score, enough to keep me chewing Stella's nickel steaks until Christmas. I took a deep breath and went all in.

"Last call boys," I said quietly. "Money and cards on the table, winner takes all."

The call went around the table, player by player.

"I'm in."

"Me too."

"As am I my dear sir, all in."

"You sure about that?"

I said nothing but laid down my cards on the table. "Read 'em and weep boys, Aces over eights."

Judging by the disgust with which my fellow players threw down their cards I knew I'd won. I leaned over to scoop in my lunch money when an ugly accent broke the magic spell.

"Ah don't think so."

I should have known this game wasn't going to end well. Yeah, it was the last hand of the night, and everybody was dog-tired and dead drunk, but in my hands were five cards that made even me sit up in a cold sweat. A hand like this would normally be winner takes all, after which I'd be laughing all the way to the bank. But this time I wasn't laughing.

I looked up to see a derringer pointed at me, a .25 calibre Colt judging by the shape of the barrel. Those things were called a joy girl's gun, a small two-shot weapon useless beyond ten feet. Most of the working girls I knew carried one in their stocking tops. Colt made them hammerless so they wouldn't snag on the way up. All it needed was a long leg or an oversize belt buckle to hide in. As he rose to his feet the great state of Texas made an appearance at his waist.

"Hey, c'mon cowboy, I won fair and square or didn't your momma teach you that a full house beats all."

"Beatin' is one thing but cheatin's another. That's something we do know about back to home," he groused. "We don't take too kindly to cheats, mister, especially the smarmy city folk kind."

"You mean like me."

"Yeah, like you, city boy."

I glanced over at the mortician. He was even paler than before if that was possible, the arms he held up waving like flags on a windy day. The other were statues, mouths wide open, eyes popping in fear.

"And what makes you think I was cheating, mister. I got three aces and you probably got none. Unless you got a straight or a flush, which I ain't seen all night, we're done here. Seems pretty simple to me. Ain't that right boys." They agreed but not very bravely.

Cowboy didn't say a word but reached down with his free hand and flipped over his hand. Two of the five were aces. "I don't know about y'all but I count five aces. Ain't there supposed to be only four in a deck?"

Damn. Of all the times for Stella to get sloppy. She was always looking for ways to cut back on her expenses, one of which was to reuse the cards for the games she set up. Looked to me like she could count to fifty-two but not in any kind of order. I had to wonder how many more fives were in the deck. I didn't want to know and wasn't about to ask.

"Look, pal, this is obviously a mistake of some kind. I know the woman who sets these things up. She musta counted wrong or something when she put out the cards."

"Counted my ass," he snarled. "You 'n' her are in this together ah kin jus smell it." The derringer was wavering as his temper rose. I didn't like the way this was going, it was still pointed at me.

We were all of us on our feet now, standing there like dummies with our hands in the air while Texas tried to decide what to do next. He figured he'd been cheated, figured it was one of us, but with only two shots he couldn't kill us all. This was going to end badly for someone and I didn't want that someone to be me.

The mortician, sweat pouring off him like rain drops, fainted. He went backwards onto the scuffed linoleum, crushing his chair on the way down and bumping the table. Cowboy turned towards him and fired blindly, the crack of the shot breaking the deadly silence. I upended the table at him, dropped down into a crouch and yanked out my hardware. The others vanished into the room next to kitchen, beyond which was the front door and freedom. Couldn't say that I blamed them much for running, it wasn't supposed to be like this. And usually it wasn't.

The table saved my life. The edge of it hit his gun arm forcing the second shot, which disappeared into the wall to my right. As he stepped back to avoid the table I pushed it over on top of him and climbed onto it, gun in hand. I had intended to have a little talk with my boy about his manners, but he tossed me and the table aside like he was swatting flies.

Fatman broke my fall. Landed on top of him with the table on top of the both of us. I couldn't see Cowboy but I did see the derringer skitter across the floor. I was really hoping he didn't have two. Then he was up and running, stomping all over us while making tracks for the front door. Heaving the table aside, I got off a couple of shots at him. Chewed a little off the door frame but that was it and then I found myself all alone with Fatman, and a sea of cash.

Stella was going to be plenty mad about tonight. I'd never known any of her games to turn like this. Considering the players involved, she'd probably lost a couple c-notes, but that wasn't the real problem. Four valuable players, and me, getting shot at and scared off was bad for business.

Those four were some of only a very few that had enough cash to play on a regular basis, and lose it calmly. Me, I couldn't afford to lose a thing, nor could she. No one in this dust bowl of a town would feed me for free as often as she did, or set me up with a game, without first paying to play.

A breeze blowing in from an open window cleared out the smoke as I tossed aside the furniture and the mortician to look for the pot. It was scattered everywhere. I almost had my first handful when someone started shouting through the open door from out in the hallway.

"Police!" the voice shouted nervously. "This is the police, I'm armed and I'm coming in! Don't move! Get your hands up!"

Not this doughboy. Grabbed all the loose cash I could and got out.

Following the breeze out the window, I flew down the fire escape. It was a rickety wooden thing that swayed dangerously as I raced for the ground. I wasn't about to spend another night downtown, it was too expensive. I'd been taken in a raid about two months ago, when one of Stella's semi-regulars ratted her out when he lost too much. The little punk had tried to go all in against an inside straight, and when I cleaned him out, he went home cryin' to momma. Which happened to be the first beat cop he could find. It cost me all my winnings plus the extra I had tucked away in my shoe just to get out in time for breakfast.

Hitting the bottom of the escape, I stopped to catch my breath, and took a quick look up to see how close the pursuit was. There wasn't any. Guess he was too busy confiscating the remains of the pot to worry about the holes in the wall, or the overly large mortician buried under all the furniture. I turned to run, got ten paces and fell flat on my face. And with good reason, there was someone in my way, just lying there in the alley.

I scrambled to me feet, yanked out my piece, and aimed it at whatever had dumped me into the gravel. Swept the alley looking for anything that might be trouble but there was only silence and moonlight. I edged slowly over to the still motionless form and nudged with it with my toe. Nothing.

My new friend was about my height and slim, wearing heels and a skirt suit, with shoulder length hair. I sighed and holstered my piece. Knelt down for a closer look, cursing my luck and wondering why me. She was lying face down in the middle of the alley in a pool of blood, still warm to the touch. I rolled her over onto her back and checked for a pulse. There wasn't one and I didn't hear any breathing when I put an ear close to her lips. Great. Just wonderful. I get away from the slowest flatfoot in town only to run into a stiff that isn't mine with her blood all over my shoes. Here I am, innocence itself for once in my life, and I could be looking at a murder rap.

I stood up and walked slowly around her, looking closely at the ground for any clue or hint of what might have happened. I could have just left her but that instinct, that inner curiosity that a drives PI, took over. It was throwing questions at me that I couldn't answer and kept pushing me to look closer. There was no case here, no clues, no witnesses, nothing, just a feeling that this wasn't what it seemed. I get this itch in my fingertips every once in a while, it's what drives me to do what I do.

The search upstairs seemed to be over, and luckily no one had thought look out the window. Guess he didn't want to complicate things by actually doing his job, and besides, he had Fatman. Cuffing him was proof enough that he had done his job, breaking up another illegal card game and managing to get an arrest. No doubt most of the pot was tucked into his boots and was going home to the wife and kids. Even cops have to eat.

Our mortician friend was probably going to spill everything, which was going to be bad news for Stella. It was going to mean a couple of phone calls and a trip to the vault in her office floor. She'd be out of action for a couple of days but at least it wasn't my fault this time. I'd be in for a week of her tossing my steak at me followed by a grubby palm held out for cash and a tip. Then she'd calm down and things would be square between us again.

My alley cat didn't seem to be much above thirty and was reasonably well off judging by her hair and clothing. What was she doing here I wondered, someone else had known, and had made sure she didn't leave. Gunshots would have woken half the neighbourhood so I figured she'd been stabbed. That made it personal. I mean you have to be close enough to count nose hairs to use a knife, and without any screams it had to have been someone she knew. So, what was someone like her doing in a place like this? That PI thing had made me curious, even when I was off the clock. Everything was suspicious and everyone was a suspect.

Even more curious was the fact that she still had her purse. Any good thug would have grabbed that, ditched the knife in the nearest sewer, and run like hell. That she still had hers made me think I'd interrupted something else, or maybe scared him off before he could finish. Either way there was no percentage in being the good Boy Scout any longer. From what I could see this had murder written all over it.

I pulled her purse from under her left arm. It was leather with a big brass snap, the narrow shoulder strap still looped over her shoulder. I popped it open, not expecting to find anything more than a little cash and some tissues. And that was as far as I got. I heard footsteps approaching from farther up the alley, along with some heated whispers. Heavy leather boots crunched slowly and carefully towards me. Was it a nosy neighbour, or was the knife hand looking to pick up where he'd left off.

A flashlight came on, momentarily blinding me. I looked up into the light.

"Police!"

I yanked her purse clear of her shoulder, tucked it under my arm and made tracks for the street, staying in the shadows until I was around the corner and gone. Footsteps followed, but they stopped at the body.

CHAPTER TWO

Murder happens it's one of the big reasons why I'm still in business. People don't get along at the best of times, but there is that certain point, that invisible line that is crossed, and when it's crossed bad things happen. Seeing her lying there like that, dead and dumped, my first instinct was to walk away. You have to, otherwise you'd go nuts.

Not that I'm saying we were murder happy in this town, but I probably saw a lot more than most, which left me a little jaded. Most of these unfortunates took a quick trip in the meat wagon to the morgue and that was the end of it. Unless it was some high society dame with a smoking .38 in her hands, downtown didn't care much. No time, no money, not enough manpower, all the usual excuses.

There was no percentage in being the good Boy Scout, you can't change dead.

Morning came soon enough and with it a blank slate between my ears. Just like the last couple of weeks, nothing and no one on my mind, never a good thing for a PI. You had to stay sharp to stay alive, and that meant casework. This was an unforgiving business, one wrong step and you stopped a bullet or pulled a long sentence. Practice didn't make perfect but it helped.

I put one of my last smokes to work to take my mind off things and do something beyond nothing. All I had going for me was cigarette smoke and silence, and the purse buried in the dust on my desk. After several turns around the room, I pitched my butt into a corner of the room, grabbed the thing, and dumped it out. It wasn't calling out to me but maybe there was something inside to make my day.

My Jane Doe was more plain than jane judging by the bag brown leather with a big brass clasp, thin shoulder strap, and just a bit of heft. Inside was a different story, bursting with paper and jewelry. It made for one big heap on my desk, but didn't add up to much of a life. I spread it all out, fingering each item carefully and giving them each a place on my desk.

Dames being what they are, there should have been a whole lot more. Change, lipstick, hankies, hairpins all the usual crap that women collect. I filed that little tidbit away and turned my attention to the papers she'd been lugging around. They were new and crisp to the touch, save for a couple that had seen better days. All were neatly folded in four, and packed carefully inside, speaking to a purpose. I snapped one open, big and green and stiff that screamed government. Seeing the word Naturalization at the top I quickly folded it back up. Another one, stiff and white, said Insurance. First time I'd smiled in weeks.

The jewelry was a different story, jammed in on top as if grabbed in a hurry. She wasn't the first to leave town with the family jewels, but it seems someone had taken exception to that. I looked it over for any markings or brand names, I knew a lot of jewelers around town, honest and otherwise. They were always happy to get their stuff back, especially before lawyers and other leeches could get their paws on it. Most of them knew their own work, but if I could find a name or a date, a couple of calls and I would be done for the day, along with a fat little finder's fee.

At first glance this was pretty chintzy stuff, dime store playthings that glittered in the morning sun but didn't add up to more than the price of a cup of coffee. A couple of pieces had the heft and quality that suggested a greater value. That meant cash, and brother did I have a need for that right now. Like I said not everyone could pay for whatever services I cared to provide. Money still made the world go around, you couldn't eat, sleep or grease a palm without it.

Cash in hand was the only thing that counted, and aside from robbing a bank, the only other money machine in town was your friendly neighborhood fence. The town was crawling with them, more so since life had gone south. If you could part with it they would pay you for it, usually pennies on the dollar. Easy money for them and no end of takers. Too many people chasing too little work meant it was a buyer's market, for everything from carats to cars. Trick was knowing who to trust, and who paid out in folding currency. Honesty among those thieves was the biggest lie of them all.

Leaving the purse and the papers on my desk, I stuffed all the jewelry into my pockets and made for the street. Breakfast was calling and Stella was in no mood to pick up my tab anymore. And with good reason, considering I was in between cases and backing three-legged nags at the track, I was tapped out. Money made the world more livable, but so did a good steak. And right now, it was all I could think of. That meant a quick trip to see a man about my waistline.

The jewelry would loosen my belt for a while, the papers I wanted to take a good second look at. My PI nose was starting to sniff something about this woman and it spelled murder and mayhem, my two favorite words. Add to that the long odds of a murder rap and things were starting to get interesting. So, the possibilities were starting to fall into place. Was she somebody's secretary, a courier maybe, a mule, some lost little lamb in with the wrong crowd? Wouldn't be the first time some adventurous skirt bit off more than she could chew.

Most of the time it was simply about life getting in the way. I had a case once where the secretary, a cute young brunette in a tight sweater, dropped dead as a doornail at her desk, no one there except her and the water cooler. I got the call because I was owed a favor, and I answered the phone when it rang.

Dragged my sorry self down to the office at the crack of dawn and stumbled into the crime scene. Helped myself to a cup of joe to sober up my thinking while surveying the scene and damn near coughed up a lung. The pot was still warm to the touch but that wasn't the problem. I drink enough of the stuff to know good from bad from paint thinner and this stuff wasn't all that bad. What I couldn't figure out was why it was giving me the heaves.

It was coming up as fast as it was going down, which wasn't doing much for my hangover or my state of mind. But it was that slight aftertaste, that same bitterness you get when you choke down bad shine that got me to wondering. Enough to get some of it checked over by a chemist friend. Rat poison he said, smiling. Who'd you piss off this time?

Not me, her. Turns out she was doing the hokey-pokey with the boss man. So when she got all cute and demanded a ring, go figure, he got cute and added a little extra to her coffeepot. Coroner said it probably took about a week, slow but steady, and very final.

Helluva thing but was it any worse than faking a burglary and doing in the wife for the insurance? There was nothing new in that either.

From a distance, we were a small town full of tall buildings, taller tales and a dark underbelly. Get closer and you could see the dark side in the broken windows and boarded up store fronts, For Sale signs plastered everywhere. When the worlds luck ran out it hit everybody hard. You went to bed one night all lovey-dovey with the wife, you woke up the next morning and you got nothing. No money, no job, and no way out. Just like someone had turned out the lights and then stolen the bulbs, it was all gone.

After that, a kind of darkness settled had over everything, swallowing hope whole and spitting out anger and misery. The streets were still full of people, but now they were hungry, broke, and angry, all trying to figure out what the hell happened. Those lucky few that still had hope, and a job, civic hacks like Mungo and Parker, hurried past them like a storm was coming, collars up and heads down, praying today would not be their last.

Me, guess I was luckier than most. I watched from the inside of Stella's café as the world outside went all to hell. The darkness sucked the life out of the place, wiping smiles off faces and turning the nice into the nasty. And the nasty did dumb things like robbery and murder, things that the law didn't allow but didn't seem to care about anymore. For a time it felt like I was the only law in town and I didn't have enough bullets.

Money was still around if you knew where to look, and if you didn't there were other ways of getting your hands on some. That's how I got to know Louie the Fat and the other local money machines. Staying in business meant taking pretty much anything for my services, and while I wasn't exactly swimming in dough, I wasn't starving either, until now. Took me a while and a few bum deals before I latched onto my particular friend and came to him exclusive. Today I had a pocketful of pretty that was going to get me ten cents on the dollar while all the other schmucks were getting three or four.

It was too early in the day for me to be walking, so I crawled into a cab and dropped a couple of rings into a sweaty palm. My man folded them into a meaty palm, cheerfully tore into the morning traffic, and belted out show tunes for the entire trip. I thought my starving brain was going to explode. All I wanted was cash and coffee and instead I got Mario Lanza's brother.

The end of the first act couldn't come soon enough. I staggered over to Fat Louie's doorstep while shaking the theatre out of my ears. Home sweet home was a pile of dingy red brick piled right smack in the center of town. No grand entrance, fancy windows, or anything else that might have been considered decorative, just a rusty black fire escape that vanished up into the darkness, and a massive steel door painted green. The neighbors must have been thrilled.

I ignored the peephole and hammered on the door. I wanted him to know who it was, and so did he. Not that he had anything to worry about. We were amigos enough for him to open up without opening up. The peephole winked, followed by a loud rattle as the door was unbolted and slowly creaked open. I pulled back my suit coat as I walked in to show that I was packing. It could stay so long as I kept it in plain sight, something not too many street side bankers allowed.

That's why Rico was there. He was the eye at the peephole and the muscle behind the door. Unlike his oversized boss, he had the ability to feed you your shoes, laces and all, should you be inclined to be less than pleasant during your visit. I waltzed in all smiles.

Down a short hallway and through a second steel door, black this time, and into the big boy's office. One very large room painted a dingy white, occupied by an enormous desk and even more enormous owner, and all lit up like an airport runway. So now I was blind as well as deaf.

Fat wasn't a word Louie liked to hear. Not in my presence, dear boy, not if you value anything in your life beyond your own tawdry physicality. He was a big man with big words, although mountain might have summed it up better. My man was a massive plug of humanity stuffed into black silk jammies, parked behind an oversized outsize desk the size of a battleship. The man knew how to live.

Besides being the poor man's banker he was also the poor

PI's library. He knew everyone and everything, or so he kept telling me. I know all and see all, my illiterate friend, ask and I shall see what cannot be seen, know what cannot be known. And then he'd rattle off something that sounded pretty impressive and usually was. The advice I could do without but the information I couldn't live without. Some days you'd think it was he and Stella running the place instead of the suits down at City Hall.

The fruits of his devious labors were piled up everywhere, covered in dust and held together by spider webs. It was all stuff he'd picked up for less than a song and most of it had no more value than a dead pigeon. Oh but of course it does he would mumble, and I own it all. Mark my words my boy, there will come a time when I shall reap the rewards of this long and hard life of mine. And it shall be warm and sandy and lined with palm trees. Hoagie?

Aside from his sparkling personality, the man was an eating machine and today was no exception. There were plates and platters everywhere, littered with crusts of bread, bits of filling and god knows what else. I sat down carefully in the one chair provided for company, one eye on Rico and the other on something furry washing up in a corner. Louie waved a tree limb of an arm like a magician, offering me a choice of whatever edibles were still available. I passed.

"Well, well, well, look what the cat dragged in," rumbled the oversized sandwich. "You must indeed be in dire straits, or did a blind man rob you again."

"Top of the morning to you too, sunshine. Is that breakfast I see or are you still working on last Christmas?"

The sandwich swallowed, wiped his mouth with a sleeve, and waved a chubby mitt at Rico. He vanished, presumably to start bringing in this week's lunch.

"Sit. Speak. Wine is a mocker, my illiterate friend. From the Bible. You should read it some time. You can read, can't you?"

"Enough with the poetry, I'm just looking for a little cash is all, not a history lesson."

"Indeed. And who is it this time. Halt? Blind? Lame?"

"No one you'd know."

"I didn't think so. Let me see dear boy, let me see what God hath wrought that you have brought."

I tossed my collection onto the only clear space on his desk. Fat fingers rifled through it with the finesse of a surgeon, assessing each piece on its look and feel. Whatever interested him went under the jeweler's loupe hanging around his neck, the rest he tossed aside like old fruit. Four pieces made the cut, the pieces I'd pegged to fill my wallet.

"Interesting little items, interesting indeed," he murmured. "Not worth a lot but worth something certainly. "

"That something better be more than a cold beer. I kinda fancy an omelet today."

"Do you indeed?"

"Yeah."

"So, what we have here my illiterate friend," he said waving his hoagie over them like a magician, "are the items of interest to you and to me. This one is a bracelet, eighteen carat gold, made for a slim wrist. Your unknown was a woman I take it, well off and presumably not able to speak for herself. She has or had a good eye, note the filigree work along the back here. It…"

"Yeah, look, the history lesson is nice but I'm kinda in a hurry."

I got a look from him that I knew only too well, the schoolteacher about to smack the rotten kid with the big mouth and even bigger attitude.

He reached behind him and pawed open the door of a black safe the size of my office. The jewelry went in and cash came out, tens as always, and only ten of them. Louie never had more than tens in the safe, ever, some kinda superstition or something. He wouldn't tell me but what did it matter, it was just his way. And I was up a C-note. "So, who is she?"

"Who's who?" I asked innocently.

"The woman you got these from," he said, smiling wickedly. "Another case gone amiss? Someone else can't afford your...ahem…low low prices?"

"Not exactly. Somebody took a dislike to her last night. A permanent one."

"Really? And you came to rescue like the good little Boy

Scout you are?"

I sat back and lit my last cigarette, tossing the burnt match onto his desk. He scowled and hastily picked up the offending object, dropping it onto the floor where Rico, finished with serving breakfast, stepped forward to grind it under his toe.

"Like I said, someone took a personal dislike to her last night. She wasn't in any condition to say much when I found her. And there's nothing in the papers this morning. I find that curious. You know what those ink boys are like, they get a sniff and out they come like wolves on a carcass. You wouldn't happen to know anything about that now would you, being the good Boy Scout and all yourself?"

"No, I would not. You know better than that," he sighed. "But I do wish you would be more careful. A fire in this place would be most unfortunate."

"What happened to her was most unfortunate."

"Ah."

"Yeah, ah. So listen, if you hear anything, maybe someone's missing, or looking, you let me know first, right?"

He nodded. I saw myself out.

Stopped for a shine, couple packs of Luckies, a mickey, and sucked in some fresh air. Didn't recognize the scent but it didn't matter, today was going to be one of those days. The siren call of a well-done steak, greasy fries, and a side of slaw, aided and abetted by the cash in my pocket, dragged me over to Stella's. Heaven on a plate to me, my usual crap to her.

In addition to her gambling and real estate rackets, she ran a little hole-in-the-wall diner that fried everything including the coffee. It was out front on one of the busier streets in town and came with its own brand of flies. Leaving without paying wasn't an option, nor was not tipping.

Except for me. Hers was one of the few places left that let me run a tab when business was slow. And I could always pick up on a rumor or two or catch the latest buzz on who was doing what to whom. She knew a lot of people, high and low, and ran the whole shebang from a payphone in the back. A coupe of calls, a mumble or two and a deal was done. All without paper, promises, or cash. And she never sold anyone out or tipped her hand to anyone. You had to respect that, if only because that hand could make bad things happen.

Maybe that's why we got along so well. She was the closest thing I had to a friend in this town and I treated her with the kind of respect you gave a live grenade. Doing what I do means I couldn't always pay and she didn't ask why it all just worked out in the end. And today was one of those days. I had enough jingle in my pocket to make up for everything and then some.

"Hey."

"Hey yourself."

She pointed to a booth in a corner and went back to her only other customer, he was the breakfast rush. I cracked open a menu and pretended to read it. Like I was interested in anything else but my usual, a little delight I called the Five Star special. That drove her nuts. No wonder you ain't never gettin' hitched, you only eat one thing. Ain't ya ever heard of fish or liver? I got a special running on veal this week. And so on. It was kinda like being married, with all of the nagging and none of the kids.

Once my money passed the scratch and sniff test coffee, black and strong, slid across the battle-scarred table top and slammed into the creamer. A large dose of that, two lumps of sugar, a splash of my fifth, and I was ready for anything. But it wasn't ready for me. I made the case that I was a paying customer and where was my meal. Apparently, the rush had slowed things a little so I got told to shut it and wait.

The décor was no raving hell. Faded sunflowers on the walls did their best to hide the fly strips while a squeaky ceiling fan fought with the cook's radio. Well-aged red leather graced the booth I was in, worn smooth and deeply furrowed. Her little slice of heaven and my second home.

Then the floor show returned, all three hundred fifty pounds of it, and threw my special at me. I didn't even wait for it to stop spinning before hacking off a great big juicy hunk and wolfing it down. She heaved herself into the seat opposite me, a cigarette jammed into her pudgy lips and started blowing smoke my way. Not a word passed between us until I was done.

"So what happened? I set ya up with a coupla losers and some cowboy or other, shoulda been simple enough. Next thing I know I got every cop in the city breathin' down my neck."

"Your cowboy friend called me out," I growled back. Breakfast was slowly filling me with the milk of human kindness but it didn't cover insulting my intelligence. "Didn't have much choice, did I? He was all set to turn me into Swiss cheese, all on account of there being too many aces in the deck. You can count, can't ya?"

"Yeah, about that. Mungo told me this morning. Guess I'm getting lazy in my old age."

"Or too big," I smirked as I lit a cigarette. "You ever consider lightening up a little. You're a walking coronary."

"That's what my second husband said just before he ran off."

"Really?"

"Really."

"Lucky him."

"So, you got cash, whatcha working on."

"Tell the truth I don't really know. You hear anything about what happened after the game was over last night? Cops say anything to you? Anybody missing? A woman maybe? Good looking, early thirties, well dressed, brunette?"

"Not a thing. All I know is Mungo and Parker came by for breakfast this morning and blew my ears off about getting shot at. You get into another fight or something? C'mon, I'm paying you enough not to do that already! Ya can't take on the whole world, just let it slide once in awhile, why dontcha. So, who is she, and why are you stuck with her?"

"Yeah, well, thing is I'm not really stuck with her, just curious is all."

"Yeah, well, don't be. I got 'nother game comin' up soon and I sure as hell don't need any more players scared off. Play nice, okay?"

"Okay, okay, I get it, be the good little boy."

"You better be. If I hear anything I'll let you know, okay?" And with that she heaved her bulk out of the booth and shuffled back to the kitchen.

"Gee thanks, I'll be just fine."

I came close to whistling as I left Stella's, but caught myself just in time. Dim memories of whistling's darker side still haunted me, no need to tempt fate.

They say payback is a bitch, and in my business, she's cast iron and unforgiving. Especially in this burned-out burg. You may lose it all and have nothing left to give, but it's the same with the next guy. He knows you still owe him from ten years back and he wants it now. When you can't or won't, even the nicest guy can show a streak of mean.

I'm old school, a debt is a debt. Might take me ten years to pay it off but that's what I do. And if I can't pay in full, a little on account. Everybody gets something, and while it doesn't bring a smile to their faces, I don't get too many doors slammed in mine. Today little miss cast iron was going to learn a lesson about forgiveness and I was going to be the teacher. I had a couple places in mind where people wouldn't be happy to see me, even with cash in hand.

Like my chemist friend Jimmy. Ran a drugstore kitty corner to my office, a corner I'd avoided lately. He's a nice guy, can't say no, but he's got a wife and kids, I'm sure she's bent his ear about me more than once. Like every single time I wander in.

Today was no different. I could feel the iciness the moment the door jangled open. She was over in a corner sweeping up but she stopped the moment I waltzed in. Didn't move a muscle and didn't take her eyes off me. Jim was friendly enough and came away from stocking shelves to pump my hand and get between me and her. Not that she could take me but I'm sure she was dying to try.

Waving off his offer of a seat and a cup of coffee, I ordered a couple packs of Luckies and a fifth of something smooth. It was nice and summery outside but the air in here was so cold I was starting to shiver. I figured I was gonna need skis to get out.

I cracked open a pack, took Jim's offer of a light, and started counting out what I owed. The smile on his face was a mile wide, hers not so much. Most of the people I deal with accept that I only pay a little at a time. He was the only one I made sure got what was coming to him as soon as I had it. Kids.

No sooner did the last bill hit the counter than did a slim brown arm reach between us and snatch the whole pile. She didn't like me, that was plain enough, but you'd think paying up would melt the ice little. Nope. I had to ski over to the front door and jangle my way out.

A couple more stops, a couple more half smiles, and I should have been all smiles myself but I just wasn't in the mood. This was business, as much as I hated to admit it, I needed them more than they needed me. They helped me out when called upon but they weren't always willing. That's why PIs are the bad pennies of the world, you can't keep strong-arming people for favors, especially the less than legal ones, and expect them to be glad to see you.

I wasn't the homebody type, the nine-to-fiver with a briefcase and an ulcer, I had to keep moving, keep myself busy. About the only recreation I took part in, besides sampling every Scotch ever made and keeping the Lucky Cigarette Company busy, was the racetrack. It was the only place where I could walk in and not worry if whispers went around the room. It was a noisy, smoky, city where the ordinary mixed with the well-heeled and no one's nose got out of joint over it. There was more money here than in most banks, and just as many broken dreams.

Maybe it was the scent of all that money or the roar of the crowd but I found a kind of comfort here. Most days I could be found leaning over the rails, soaking it all up like a sunny day on a warm beach. Peace and quiet didn't come easy to me, too many demons on the inside trying to fight their way out. Maybe that's why my knuckles never healed and I ran a tab at the gunsmith. Bullets weren't cheap.

Horse racing was supposed to be the sport of kings but around here anyone with a pulse could get in on it. There was just something about a live body running around a track that grabbed people like nothing else. It was as if their lives depended on that one good bet, that winning would somehow make it all better, bring back the sunshine and roses. Maybe so, but there were others who saw it as an opportunity to grab all that sunshine and make it their own.

Which maybe explained why the first person I saw was my old friend Texas.

CHAPTER THREE

I was up in the stands throwing money through a betting window when I heard that certain voice, the one you don't forget because it tried to kill you. It was a mob scene as it always was up here, sweaty bodies mixed with cigar and cigarette smoke and hoarse voices, plunking down their lunch money in hopes of winning dinner. Which for most of us meant eating dust because that's all we ever won.

I couldn't exactly place him at first, what with everything going on. The fifth race was about to start and there was a rumour that the fix was in for the number four horse, Piano Boy. Could be he was a ringer getting in some race time for some quick cash and a chance at hitting the bigs down south. Belmont was the word of the day, so naturally everybody and his dog was lining up to bet gramma's grave on him. Made the odds longer but when did that ever worry me.

Then I saw his hat, the same big, ten-gallon lid he'd been wearing when he rose up to dispense his form of justice the other night. Big movie style thing with a snakeskin band and a feather. It was bobbing up and down not twenty feet from me but it might as well have been a quarter mile there were so many bodies in the way. It was all I could do to get a little closer without being trampled or mugged.

He picked that moment to start moving so I did likewise, pushing through the crowd while keeping an eyeball glued to the feather. We travelled the length of the grandstand, shot down an exit to ground level, and then bee-lined for the stables out in the back. And he wasn't alone, he had some wiggle-hipped floozy on his arm, and a coupla losers with slicked back hair and cheap suits in hot pursuit.

We strolled down a broad stretch of open area called the Concourse, a tree lined avenue jammed to the rafters with guys and dolls out for a good time. Even if you were lining your shoes with newspaper to cover the holes, right here is where you wanted to be. Winning wasn't the thing; to see and be seen was. There was money here and lots of it, you could smell it. And see it, cars by the dozen parked every which way, all shiny and new, and every colour of the rainbow.

To the left of the Concourse was the stabling for the horses and a fenced-in paddock. A bunch of horses and their trainers were hard at it, even on a sunny day like today. To the right was an open-air picnic spot swimming in cheap beer and coney's. Adding to the human mix on the Concourse were more horses, with their jockeys on board, going to and from the racetrack. It was a sea of humanity and horseflesh so thick not even Moses could have parted it.

A long march to wherever they were going, but they were easy enough to follow. I didn't know what I was getting into but that was half the fun of being a PI. Boy Scouts had to be prepared for whatever life threw at them, a PI had to be prepared for whatever life shot at them. Bet there wasn't a badge for that.

The march ended at a long low shed at the east side of the Paddock. Didn't look any different from any of the other buildings except for the two goons standing guard over the door. I pulled up short and grabbed a wandering stable-hand.

"What gives," I asked, nodding at the building in question. "Lot of people going in there. Anything I should know?"

"You a cop?" He murmured.

"No," I said, stuffing a five into his shirt pocket. "Just curious is all. Friend of mine went in there but he clams up when I ask what's cooking. That a Shriner convention or something?"

"Oh, hell no," he drawled. "Supposed to be for the vet but they all got kicked out a while ago. They got a game in there, a real big one. Lotsa women too but mostly it's the cards, ya know. See, them slicks come in here all day, play all night. They make a lotta noise, kinda spooks the horses some, makes 'em a little skittish, don't run so good some of them."

"That a fact? Any way I can get in there? Just wanna see if I can surprise my friend."

"Long as you got cash they let anybody in."

"So what's with those two," I asked, nodding at the two fullbacks.

"Who, them? That's just in case some loser comes back and causes trouble. I seen what they do and it ain't pretty. Best stay away is my advice."

"I'll keep it in mind. Thanks pal."

And with that I slowly wandered over, giving them both a good look. Their suits bulged in all the right places. Other than eyeballing the better-looking skirts, all they did was make sure the door stayed closed.

Entry was easy enough, I joined a couple of those skirts and their boyfriends and wandered on in like I owned the joint. A piece of this action and I coulda retired in a week. The place was packed, the air thick with smoke, the shriek of half-loaded women having a good time, and the roar of their menfolk having a better one.

All around the outside of the room were tables, chairs, booze, broads and the flash of cash, in the centre a pair of monster roulette tables. They stood at least thirty players with twice as many more leaning over their shoulders. The croupiers were doing their best to keep things under control and see that the balls spun the right way, but there were a lot of hands trying to help out. Everywhere someone was betting on something, waving fistfuls of cash and yelling to beat hell.

I picked up a lonely scotch along the way, helped myself to an equally lonely silver cigarette case and lighter, and made my way to the very back. Lit up what turned out to be a quality smoke, eyeballing the scene looking for my man. Back here it was a little quieter if only because poker requires finesse and not so loud a voice. Two tables over I could see the feather, the hat, and the loudmouth cardsharp from Texas. Judging from all the paper in front of him he was sitting in on some very high stakes poker, and winning. A slim arm slid around my waist and pulled a nice warm body up close to mine.

She finished my drink for me and asked if I had a light for a lady. I said no but snapped open the case and offered her one anyways. She lit up using my new lighter and exhaled sharply, nodding at the game in front of us.

"Interested?"

"In what, you or them?"

"Both."

"Neither, just curious is all."

"Oh" and she made to leave.

"Not so fast, honey. Couple questions and the case is yours. Deal?"

She took the case without comment and stuffed it into a very intimate place.

"So whadda ya wanna know?" she mumbled. Charming, looked like a china doll; spoke like Little Orphan Annie.

"So, what's with all this? Last time I checked booze was legal again. I figured places like this were all shut down."

"Nah, legal's got limits but this place don't. Bet 'til you're broke, that's the rule."

"And what about you, what's your play in all this."

"Anything you want, honey, any way you want it. Hell, I ain't seen the sun for a week. Don't need to. Got everything I need right here, 'cluding all the booze I can drink. You got somethin' particular in mind, I got friends."

"Pass, but who's he?" I said innocently, nodding at the feather.

"Don't know, but that don't mean nuthin'. Anybody can just wander in and help themselves. You sure you ain't...."

"Sorry honey, just a little information is all I'm after." A powerful, bullet-scarred arm, circled her waist and pulled her in nice and tight. Kinda felt good having a warm body this close and she didn't seem to mind. She snuggled right up close and actually put her head on my shoulder.

We stood there the two of us like we were an old married couple, watching the kids going off to college. She might have dozed off for a bit, but it didn't matter to me. At least she wasn't trying to stick me with something sharp.

She came back to life after a short catnap and palmed a pair of smokes out of her new case, one-handed. Neat trick. Took a couple puffs, passed me one, and then started up where we'd left off.

"So, who's who," I asked. "Anybody you know?"

She took a quick sweep of the scene before answering. A pro did that, the good kind.

"Most of 'em are locals, play all the time. No big whoop any of 'em. "Cept that big guy," she said, nodding at Texas. "Ain't seen him before. I read 'im as a player, but not all that good. He keeps makin' signs like he's got friends at the table, probably those slicks at the end." Now this was a real pro at work. Might make for a good partner if I wasn't so lousy at keeping them alive.

"Let me guess, those two slim jims, right? Mook A and Mook B?"

"Yep."

And then I heard those all too familiar words.

"I don't know about y'all but I count five aces. Ain't there supposed to be only four in a deck?"

The noise was so loud I didn't think them fightin' words registered with half the players, but they registered with me. I nudged my escort.

"There another way out of here?"

"Over there, just past the can. You going somewhere?"

"Nope, but you are. It's gonna get real ugly in here, real quick. Best you scram while you can."

Warm air kissed my left ear along with her lips. "Tell Sandy Willie says hi." And then she was gone, out of my arms as smooth as silk. I stared after her. Sandy? She knew Sandy?

And then all hell broke loose in front of me.

The idea was to step up to the table and catch the eyes of Texas. I wasn't sure what his reaction was gonna be but I wanted to rattle him a little, let him know I was onto him. And if my presence was enough to cost him a hand or two, so much the better. Teach him a lesson about crossing a stranger in a strange town. My town.

Now, it was all I could do not to get trampled in the rush. It was like a Chinese fire drill, bodies flying in all directions, all yelling to beat hell. In between the bodies, I could see my man, and he didn't seem to be in a hurry to leave. He was one cool customer, making sure his back was covered and his money in his pockets before he joined in the rush. His two friends had taken cover behind the upended table, manicured fingers shooting out to grab cash in between the flying feet.

And that's when it got interesting. In the middle of all the chaos, with me standing around waiting for the tide to go out so I could cross the beach safely, he saw me. There was that look on his face that only my best friends get when they see me coming. The motion was so smooth I almost didn't see it, but he managed to palm his derringer and get a shot off at me. Didn't hit anything but now the crowd had something else to scream about.

I returned the favour but in that split second he stepped back into the crowd and disappeared out the back way. Not so his two slims, they were on their knees stuffing whatever they could grab into their pockets, all of it cash and none of it theirs.

Next thing Mook A knew there was a brown leather brogan crushing his left hand. He yelped in pain, looked up and found himself looking cross-eyed down the barrel of my still smoking friend. His one hand went up, followed by the other as I stepped back.

Mook B had vanished.

"Where'd he go?" I asked.

"That dumbass," he said pointing to Mook B's last known position. "Long gone I bet, probably the train station if I…"

"Not him, chump, the other one, the big guy from Texas, where is he."

"Him I don't know. All we were supposed to do was grab the cash and meet up with him later and split things. See, thing is…." And that's as far as we got because the two fullbacks were about to join the party and they didn't seem too happy about it. They weren't waving iron but judging by how their suits fit they didn't have to. One punch from the fists they were waving would be more than enough. I let the last of the crowd take the lead.

Outside there was no sign of my boy, just a fence a short distance away and beyond that a field of grass waving in the afternoon breeze. The ground was littered with cigarette butts and cigar ends but no signs of life. Found a well-worn path that went around the corner and along the south side of the building back towards the Concourse. Nothing. He must have had a car waiting.

Walked back to the Concourse on the slim hope that I might see that ten-gallon flag a second time. But no such luck. It was a mob scene, hundreds of bodies jammed every which way and all yapping away to beat hell. Toss in some horses struggling against the tide to reach the paddock and I couldn't have found my man if he'd been waving at me. Tossing my race tickets to the wind, I lit up a Strike and grabbed a beer off a guy pushing through the mob carrying a full tray. He didn't even notice he was so intent on staying upright. Not my worst day at the track.

Stopping to check on the office mail should have convinced me to listen to my instincts more often. It's that hazy feeling you get when you know something's gonna happen but you don't know what or when. Trouble is, it comes and goes, so if you ignore it bad things can sometimes happen, quickly. My gun hand was in the act of pulling out a fistful of bills I wasn't going to pay when I acquired two large shadows on each side of me, both grabbing an elbow. Feeling that subtle nudge from a barrel pressed against my ribcage I relaxed and let the bills go.

They didn't say anything, they didn't have to, something snub-nosed shoved into your ribs is message enough. That being said, one shadow I can handle, it's not always pretty, but two means come along quietly. Somebody, somewhere wanted to say hello. Not all that unusual, PIs tend to get under a lot of collars, and they tend to have long memories. Most of them don't like to say hello a second time, they prefer to shoot.

We travelled quickly up the stairs and down the corridor to my office. They used my nose to open the door, dragged me in, relieved me of my piece, and tossed me into my armchair. I sat back, lit up a Strike and prepared for what was to come. I got it slapped from my lips after just one puff.

Now I'd never seen these two gentlemen before but they seemed to know me, or at least what I was intending. The bigger of the two, a bald size 48 with a barrel chest, stumped over to my desk, grabbed the purse and started jamming everything into it. His partner, a pasty-faced beanpole with slicked back hair and a pencil moustache stood over me, arms crossed, a .38 gripped tightly in his right hand. He was the non-smoker.

Since neither of them seemed to be in a conversational mood, I broke the ice.

"Something I can do for you boys?"

"Shaddup," growled Beanpole. "And don't touch nothin' and leave your hands where I can see 'em."

"This everything?" asked Baldy, from over his shoulder.

"What am I, your mother, take a look around," groused Beanpole.

It took Baldy about ten seconds to give the place the once over twice and shrugged his shoulders. "Ain't nothin' else I can see."

"Okay, boys, I get the picture," I said with a smirk. "This means you know something about what happened the other night. Friend of yours, girlfriend maybe? I gotta say I'm a little hazy on the details. Was it you that stuck her?" I asked, staring up at Beanpole. "Or was it your pal over there, the one with the purse fetish."

"Shaddup!"

"Just trying to be polite. Not used to having guests, especially big ugly ones."

Baldy took that personally. He came back to where I was sitting, shoved Beanpole aside, and held the purse up to my face. "I'm askin' you, laughing boy, is this everything?"

"You tell me, you've had a look around, or did you forget about the upstairs. Most people do. Thing is…"

"Shaddup!"

"Now look, why don't you boys tell me what this is all about and maybe we can work something out." Never hurts to ask, well not all the time, but I had to know who they were working for. Since I knew most everybody in town with a crooked bent, the name would tell me how much trouble I was in, and if I could get out of it in one piece.

All I got was a crack across the chin. I took that to mean that talking time was over. Now it was going to get interesting. Baldy threw the purse on the desk and grabbed me by the lapels, lifting me half out of my chair. Up close, his face was no prettier than the rest of him.

"I asked you a question! Is this everything?"

"Ask your mother, she's got a purse too, right?"

He didn't much care for that remark either. He threw me back into my chair hard enough to snap my spine. I could see the next one coming but I didn't wait for it. I leapt up and charged into him, driving my right shoulder into his gut. We shot across the room

like two line-backers on a first and ten, landing pretty hard in the
corner, me on top of him and swinging to beat hell. I got in a couple
of good ones before he threw me off and got in a couple himself.
That's when Beanpole got in the way, waving his gun around like he
was actually going to shoot something.

"All right, that's enough! Break it up, break it up!" yelled
Beanpole. And to my surprise the big ugly one did exactly that,
stopping in mid-swing and climbing off what was left of me.

The office door chose that moment to slam open and admit
my next door neighbour, Mrs. Chen, waving a piece of paper and
yelling to beat hell herself. Beanpole jacketed his gun and forced a
smile. Baldy made like a statue and froze in mid punch. My lucky
day.

"I hear noise! I know you here! You owe money! You pay!"
The sweetest words I'd ever heard. No doubt I owed her a few bucks
from somewhere but she'd picked a helluva time to collect. I would
have hugged her but my ribs weren't in the mood.

If there is such a thing as a sweet little old lady, she ain't it.
At all of five foot nuthin' she was little, and old, but definitely not
sweet. I had two neighbours, a quiet little schmuck downstairs who
pretended to be a tailor, and her. My office was a one room corner
on the second floor while the rest was her laundry operation. She ran
her operation, and occasionally me, just like my old sergeant had run
everybody, hard-nosed and tough minded.

That she had some kind of soft spot for me surprised a lot of
people. From the moment I'd showed up she had done her very best
to mother the crap out of me. It became her life's work to make sure
I was at least dressed and pressed, if not sober. And all it took was
me tossing a couple of deadbeats down her fire escape a coupla
times.

It was no secret that I didn't like paying bills, mainly
because I couldn't. Most didn't try to collect, but those who did took
their chances, fifty-fifty, it was cash or a fist. It was kinda the same
with her. The paint wasn't even dry on my door before a couple of
locals had wandered in to see what was new and exciting in the
laundry business. What they wanted was to offer her a protection
service, for cash. Protection from what they weren't too specific, but

it didn't protect them from me.

I don't like shakedowns at the best of times, the way I see it you gotta earn your own way in this life. Which doesn't include beating up little old ladies, even iron-fisted ones like her. Once I got involved all it got them was a free trip down the fire escape. A couple more trips over that first week and I was her friend for life.

"Why, hello Mrs. C, glad you could drop by! Say, I'd like you to meet some friends of mine," I said pointing out my two new compadres. "Boys, this is my neighbour, a sweet little old lady with a memory like an elephant. Never forgets a thing, like where she's been or who she's just met. Does laundry too, and a damn fine job if I do say so myself. Just look at these cuffs," I said, pulling back one of my coat sleeves. "Now that's quality workmanship. So, how about it boys, you got anything needs doing?"

They took one look at her, back at me, and then scrambled out the door without so much as a goodbye.

"Who those two? Never see before! When you pay me! I do good work, you promise me cash last month! I want now!"

I was slow getting up. More things hurt than should have, my own fault for not thinking anyone might take an interest in my dead friend. How long had it been, a day maybe, and already things were in play? I found that interesting, almost as much as the purse that still sat on my desk. In their haste, the boys had left it behind.

Put a smoke to my lips, exhaling loudly, trying to ignore the insistent beady eyes with the outstretched palms, glaring at me in silence.

"Hey! What wrong with you! You got cash or no?" Another deep draw and then I fished out my wallet. She left the way she had come in, the last of my new-found wealth clutched tightly in her tiny little paws. Shot my iron home, picked up the purse and looked at it a little more closely. Why was this little thing suddenly so important, I wondered? Enough to get me beat up just for having it in my hands.

I continued with this train of thought while chowing down on my usual at Stella's. As always, my favourite cook and bottle washer groused loudly at learning that I was broke again and wanted my tab re-upped. But you just paid me you big dummy, what'd you do, drink it all again, was her standard opening line. No, just the thought of your smiling face was more than I could stand. Just gimme my usual and clam up, will ya?

My house, my rules, she would reply, you don't pay you don't eat. And then she would
sing out to the cook and dinner was on its way. Lovely woman but anyone married to her would have to be crazy, or a saint. I fired a few questions at her in between bites, thinking maybe she might know something. She knew a lot of things about a lot of things, kept her chubby mitts in a lot of different pies, which is how she had survived when so many others had folded up their tents. What am I your secretary, I gotta do all your work and feed you for free? Hurry up and eat, I got a line-up to deal with, this to a café empty except for me. I was pretty sure it wasn't the food that was keeping the crowds at bay.

As my old gran used to say, begin at the beginning and the end will come to you. Fine old lady, all grey haired and churchified, but didn't know from nothing if it wasn't in the Bible. Growing up it was just me and her and the cat. Grampa wasn't in the picture for long, he drank his pension to death. Then the shooting started over there and I was off as fast as I could go. Not that I didn't appreciate her putting me up for all those years but I'd had enough of Sunday school, and regular school for that matter. I wanted out of there, wanted to see some of the real world.

All these years later and I still remembered that one piece of advice out of the thousands of others she had fired at me. The good book doesn't exactly cover the PI business but it was a reminder of what good PIs do, dig up what you can, sniff the wind, and follow the trail.

Easy enough if you know where to start and what to look for. Me, I was somewhere in the middle with no idea where to go next. To make matters worse there was someone else on this trail who did know, and was waiting for me to catch up. Or was it to take point. Those kinds of meetings never ended well and I was in no hurry. It didn't mix well with curiosity.

I put myself back in that room, looking out the window Texas had jumped out of. It gave me a good look at the alley where

I'd found my latest client, as good a place as any to pick up a scent. I pulled a couple mickeys out from under the sink, broke out the pages of the latest rag, and saluted the setting sun, one pull at a time.

Sunset was one of those moments in time when everything went silent, if only for a second or two. No sirens, no church bells, all was quiet on the western front and all was at peace. A second later and everything changed, and not for the better. The dark of night hid a lot of sins, according to Gran, and it covered this burg's sins like the holiest blanket on earth. All that was nice and good was home and having a nice hot dinner while the rest of us came to out to play.

That's what I was hoping for, the criminal element, like everybody else, was a creature of habit. Kill or rob in one particular place and get away with it and that place became the place for a time. Back for more until the supply of easy marks ran out or the cops got wise and beefed up patrols.

I'd seen this before, and had it pay off more than once. The thing was not to charge in and grab a lapel, but follow along behind nice and quiet and see what was what, and who. The who was a surprise sometimes, but they were just as guilty.

So, I stretched out on a couple chairs right beside the window and tried to count the stars but they kept getting lost in the smoke from my Luckies. A couple of hours into the darkness and I'd already heard more screams and gunshots than I had fingers and toes, none of it enough to be of any interest. Which told me that her death was no random act or some slasher out for a quick hit and a hot meal.

Somebody did her in. Here. Which meant somebody knew she was going to be here, and probably knew what she was carrying. Just my luck I showed up when I did, not soon enough to save her, and too soon for whoever it was to claim his prize and beat it. And no chance of me following them anywhere.

Maybe alleys had a quota on death and maybe mine was done because no one and nothing moved all night. Even the rats stayed home. My only consolation was that I was able to kill a lot of stuff that was bad for me and still stand up. It got to the point where I was ready to stick my head out the window and start shouting at the moon. Maybe that would get someone's attention, or just get me shot.

Long towards dawn I figured I'd had enough, staggered down the back stairs yet again and over to the scene of the crime. Only to bump into the flatfoot who'd been the only thing I'd seen wandering around the whole night. Last thing I needed was for him to get all official and pull me over for a quick frisking and a ride downtown. Luckily, he paid more attention to my inability to stand still for long, finally wishing me a good day, and quickly moving on, marvelling at how late the drunks were out tonight. True, except I wasn't drunk, just warm and fuzzy all over and looking around for clues, or anything else interesting. I wandered out of the alley.

That's when I bumped into Whitey Laroche. He was getting a shine on a pair of boots that could have doubled as small trucks. A great big goof was Whitey, blond haired, muscled, as full of life as anyone had the right to be, and with all the brains of a chicken. He could bench press a bus but couldn't bring himself to hurt a fly.

Which made him the perfect numbers runner, too big to tackle without an army and too dumb to ever think of skimming the fortune in his pockets. More cash passed through his hands in one day than most banks in a week. Couple of local bookies and at least one house of ill repute had him on the payroll. He was probably getting ready to make a run when I came cross him at a shine stand around the corner from the scene of my crime.

"Whitey, that you?"

He looked up, all of it suspicious. "Ya, who wants ta…Hey Tone, hiya!"

"Hey yourself." I poured myself into the chair beside him, and let the man do his magic on my brogans. Whitey was bent right over inspecting the results on his, trying to see his reflection in his toes.

"So, what're you doing slumming around here, last I heard you were over to 5th avenue handling the White Pass boys." They were a bunch of local toughs that hung out at a diner called the White Pass, famous for its big burgers and lack of colour in its patrons.

"No, I mean yeah I was, but they got busted last week.

Buncha coppers turned it over and threw the ol' man in the slammer. One of his girls got beat up real bad a while ago, but he didn't do nuthin' about it. She went home cryin' to some big-time lawyer she knows and next thing you know they get hit."

"So, what's up with you, they get you, too?"

"Nah," he grinned. "I was out making calls when they went in. I still got all the money. Here, want some?"

CHAPTER FOUR

He pulled a fistful of cash out of his pants pocket. All I could see were twenties and trouble. Somebody, somewhere was going to want that back, and I didn't want to be the guy trying to collect it. He tossed one of them to the shiner who all but kissed his feet in return. A month's work in one bill.

"I'd go easy on that if I was you," I said quietly. "Somebody's gonna want it back and I don't wanna be the guy picking up the pieces, know what I mean?"

"Yeah I know," I was just funnin' with ya. I'm givin' it all to his ol' lady down to the diner soon's as I'm done my boots. She runnin' things now."

"Good idea. So, listen, you been running around here lately, last couple weeks, right? Hear anything? Maybe about a dame, real looker, some kind of trouble maybe? You ever run any paper for anybody?"

"Me, nah, I mean I'm strictly cash, that's all I'm good for, leastwise that's what they tell me, I don't do no paper."

Running paper was a lot different from running numbers or anything else cash related. I was working on the idea that maybe my client was running papers for someone, which, unlike my pal here, required a certain amount of guile. If he got caught with cash in his pants, Whitey might get off with a fine or even a slap on the wrist, depending on who was doing the arresting. A lot of flatfoots were like lawyers, a monthly payoff got a lot of small timers back on the streets before the cuffs ever came off. No formal arrest, no bail, no loss of time and money.

Government paper was different. It was a crime to make it, steal it, or even just have it in your hands. It was around if you knew who and had the money but get caught with that stuff in your hot little hands, and no payoff was big enough. Guys like Whitey were too big and too obvious to be carriers, so your uptown types, broke and hungry, got the call. Who would ever suspect the society dame with diamonds on her fingers or some dandy in pinstripes. Which might explain my client.

A couple more questions and he was on his merry way,

showing off his shine like a kid with a new toy. Me, I was pretty much done. That second mickey was starting to work its magic, so I took myself home for the night, checking for the mail a whole lot more carefully this time. My office door wouldn't open, no matter how much I pleaded with it, so I sacked out in the hallway.

The light of dawn hit like a searchlight hunting the shadows for a con on the lam. A dawn so bright even the blind wore sunglasses, but I was too brain dead to care. It had been a long night of nothing. It happens. You play the odds, hoping for that lucky roll that'll get you into the game. But they're always long odds, with no guarantee of anything beyond a massive hangover and a stiff back. But this wasn't my office.

It was the shock of cold water exploding all over my face that finally kicked me awake. Damn near gave me a heart attack. Coffee, strong and black, forced its way in, a gallon of it that managed to climb over my lips before the rest of my brain came to.

When I was finally able to pry my eyelids open, all I could see was Mrs Chen. We were nose to nose, her beady little eyes giving me the once over like I was some kinda patient with a mystery disease. A large bowl of soup sat in my lap, hot to the touch and full of noodles. It was the fuel that fired the Chen clan, a secret they were always willing to share with me. Hugged that thing tighter than my first girl.

I sat for who knows how long, in a corner of their kitchen, wondering how I got here, and guzzling their liquid cure all. The place was a madhouse, steamy and sweaty, people and laundry flying in all directions, all of it in very loud Chinese. Didn't know all the players, hell I didn't even know what time it was, but that was of no import. Laundry, like time, waited for no man, especially for those particular uptown schmucks who wanted just so much starch in their shirts and a razor crease in their pants. And wanted it right the hell now. It was a wonder the Chens ever slept, let alone had time to feed a deadbeat neighbour like me.

I think it was long towards noon when I finally mustered up enough courage to try standing up. A couple of deep breaths, a shake of the noggin, and I was back in the land of the living, for which I thanked them many times over. I saw myself out and back to my life, theirs was crazy enough without me in it. I had a case that needed solving and the trail was getting colder by the second.

It was a cleaner and mostly sober me that picked up that dusty black thing on my desk and phoned Stella. I sucked back an entire smoke while holding the receiver at arms length to hear what she had to say. The woman spit more words at me than a dictionary, but I was off the hook for the other night. Sure, the boys in blue had raided the game but Stella's friends hadn't made any statements, on or off the record. It was rough for her and bad for them but good for me, I still had a place at her table.

That left the field clear for me to continue my investigation, but there were no witnesses other than yours truly. I was pretty sure Stella wasn't going to release her client to me, and without that all I had were Mungo and Parker. They were just kids and jobs like theirs came from connections that were hard to make and harder to replace. They could place me elsewhere at the time of the murder, but they weren't about to, not even for me.

So where did that leave me? She had looked to be in her early thirties, short hair, well dressed. Didn't recognise the face but I did note a certain style in her clothing. Very well cut, form fitting, expensive looking. And not wearing any jewellery, not even a ring, just what was in her purse. All of which painted a picture of a past life and maybe a clue as to why she was dead. That was for me to figure out still.

Not so the guy who'd sent Baldy and Beanpole. He already knew why. Guess I was getting a little too close for comfort, but his two goons had missed the mark. The jewellery was long gone but I still had all the papers she'd been carrying around. Sometimes luck is where you find it and today it was looking out for me.

Next up, her purse, plain black leather with a brass clasp and thin leather shoulder strap, no big whoop. Most of the women I know, the live ones, treat these things like bank vaults, keeping all their little secrets locked inside. Until they end up dead somewhere and some shmuck like me comes along and cracks the combination.

First thing to catch my eye was the crisply folded sheet of heavy green paper I'd glanced at before. I knew what that was even before I picked it up. To be a citizen in this dustbowl you had to be born here or be let in by someone official. And just plain crazy to stay here. Lucky for me guns still fired bullets into the wrong bodies.

Most civilised countries, including this one, had government departments that handled things like Taxes and Immigration. Nothing more than a bunch of chair bound do-nothings with the power of life and death in their hot little hands. They could kick you out if you so much as looked at them the wrong way, a death sentence for many because going back wasn't always possible.

And like every other swivel servant, they had their hands out. One hand took in whatever green was folded into it, while the other hand gave out a certain type of green in return. This one, the one in my hand, all shiny and new, was all signed and sealed but not yet delivered. Made you an instant person, with a nice new name on it that was not your own. Made it real easy to get lost or not be found, depending. This one was just that, all filled out except for the name.

My new client had life insurance, a standard policy that cost twenty-six bucks. Again, all filled out except for a name. A driver's license, stamped and ready to go, but no name and no car keys or parking slip. A ticket for a raffle on a fur choker for some local parish church, a handful of postcards of the local scenery, and a blank Birth Certificate, the kind you can pick up at any stationery store. Again, stamped and ready to go, but no name.

Sitting back I lit up another Lucky, blowing more smoke all over the stuff in front of me. Because that's just what this was, smoke. Somebody, somewhere was in dire need of a new identity and she just happened to be carrying one. A lot of guys in town could set you up with this kinda stuff but you had to know which ones to trust, which ones weren't going to take your money and run, or worse yet finish the job and double their fee. Finding the right guy took dough and a whole lotta luck.

I didn't recognise the handiwork, it was mostly typewritten, and the signatures were a swirl that could have been anybody's. The clue was the paperwork itself, the quality pointed to only a very few that did this kind of work. Trouble is they weren't about to let go a name if I started in on them, they were tight with each other and if one clammed up so would the rest. Then the smoke cleared and I smiled, something I didn't make a habit of.

Insurance agents, they had access to all kinds of paper, and as big a need for cash as anyone else. More so because they had a few more wheels to grease. The real insurance wasn't the policy but the cash that paid for it. Anybody and his mother could sell you a policy, just try collecting on it. Accidents didn't happen, a bullet hole was natural causes, and a missing person, well, wasn't missed for long. Helluva racket and all of it legal.

Looking at her policy, I had to laugh because I knew the dumb schmuck. We'd crossed paths before, and he was kind enough to remind me by putting his name to the policy with a big blue label.

It was a couple of years back, and right from the get go he was in the middle of it. Wifey wanted out because hubby beat her, so she goes and gets herself a legal eagle. Hubby then hides all the expensive stuff, fakes a robbery, and files an insurance claim for all the cheap crap. Come court time guess who gets the last laugh, because the paperwork is in order and she can't prove a thing. Judge throws the case out.

But she's got enough smarts, and cash, to get my attention and send me to where the treasure's buried. Next thing you know I'm kicking down a door one block down and two floors up. Scared the beejezus out of some sweet young thing modelling the jewellery, and little else. She points the finger at hubby, grabs her clothes and scrams. The insurance agent suddenly coughs up the original forms, and claims hubby faked everything, including his signature. Wifey gets her due, the agent gets his cut, and hubby gets five years.

The mastermind behind it all was J.G. Vance of Vance Insurance, Insurance of All Kinds. He'd worked both sides of the street on that case, advising them both what to do next and scooping up a fat little fee for every second of his time. Smart and expensive. Didn't I say it took all kinds?

Last time I saw him he was dancing it up at a sketchy little place, the Delta, with his inky paws all over some scared little thing. I ignored them both until she threw me this look, something Sandy had taught me to be aware of. If you see that look, step up, she needs you. Lucky for her I wasn't too fond of her dance partner. I work hard enough for my dough without my client telling me she's got to cut my fee because some insurance slug's holding a pen to her head.

I grabbed him by the collar and hauled his ass down to the john where we had a brief discussion on morals. Sent her home in a cab, which he ever so graciously paid for. So, you can imagine the look on his face when I come strolling in and plant myself in his best chair.

"So, where is she," I asked, trying not to smile too loudly.

"I ought to have you arrested for what you did," he mumbled. "I still got a tooth needs a filling because of you."

"Yeah, well, pick on someone your own size next time. Preferably when I'm not around. I got enough to do these days without keeping you on the straight and narrow."

"That's none of your business. What do you care anyways, she a friend of yours?"

"Can't say, but it might be wise to lay off the young ones. I'd hate to have to discuss it with you again."

"No kidding!"

"No kidding. Ever seen this before?" I laid out the insurance policy right under his nose, taking care to smooth out the wrinkles. He caught a glimpse of the folded Naturalisation paper before I shoved it back in my pocket. His interest in my presence perked right up.

"It's an insurance policy."

"Good guess. And it's yours, got your name on it and everything."

"Yeah, so, I do them all the time. What's it to you."

"Any idea who it's for? Anybody in particular?"

He picked it up and looked it over, turning a paler shade of white.

"Not a clue."

"How about these."

He sat back and watched while I laid out all the other papers. "Curious thing about all this is that it came from one person. And she's dead. And there's no name on any of it so I have no idea who she was. And that's what I'm trying to find out, who she was, so I can give this all to her family. If she's got one."

"How very noble of you. If as you say she's dead, why beat

the proverbial dead horse. Just call it case closed and go home. Why bother me with all this," he quipped.

"Can't do that. It kinda goes like this. I find a body in an alley, I ask a coupla questions, a coupla goons pay me a visit, I get interested. What's it all about I wonder, who else is involved I ask myself. I do a little poking around in her purse and what do I see, the name of an old friend. So, I figure what the hell, I'll pay him a little visit, see if he knows anything. So, any of this ring any bells?"

"Purse snatching is it, doesn't seem your style. Little down on your luck, are you? Sorry friend but I can't help you."

"Well, see, here's the thing. I'm just trying to be the good little boy scout and give her folks a break. I mean the insurance gotta be worth something, right? It's paid for, right? Only thing is I still don't know who because all the pages are blank."

He followed my pointing finger and examined the policy carefully from a distance, afraid to touch it in case it had leprosy. Judging by his reaction, outwardly calm but sweating like he had malaria, he knew the score.

"Not my problem if she forgot to fill them out. Happens all the time. People are always in such a hurry these days. You wouldn't believe what I have to go through to get the insurance company to honour one of these."

"Like this one, maybe?"

"Now look, I've been very patient up to this point but now you're starting to try mine. I still don't know what this has to do with me but I'm going to have to ask you to leave. I have a very important client coming in a minute and he doesn't like to be kept waiting."

"He know anything about this? Maybe I should stick around and ask him myself." I sat back, lit up a smoke and blew it at him. His reaction was to shake even harder.

"Look, friend, what help can I really be to you? Trust me, just close the case and walk away. That's what I would do if I were you." He folded his pudgy pink fingers under his chin and took a deep breath. "Now if it's money you want, I'm sure we can come to some arrangement, for an old friend."

"As long as I leave things alone, right?"

"Would a hundred be a help? Two?" he queried, eyebrows raised.

I leaned forward, blowing smoke all over his desk, pointing at the policy again. "Look, this thing has a number on it. Can't you track it down or something? You must have notes or records of some kind."

"No, I don't."

So JG was a lousy bookkeeper, what else was new. I didn't think he'd tell me anything but that wasn't the point. Lighting a fire under his kiester just might get someone else's attention. I wasn't looking forward to another friendly visit, but I figured if it was important enough somebody somewhere would make contact again. I smiled at the thought. Yeah, I'd be ready this time, really ready.

"All right, I can see I've taken up enough of your time. Wouldn't want you to miss out on a paying customer. I know what that's like."

I butted out my smoke on his desktop and got up to leave. JG put his hands flat on the insurance form like he was preparing to heal it somehow and make her name magically appear. I tugged it out from under his manicured fingernails, folded it carefully, and put it into my jacket pocket. His eyes narrowed and his mouth squared but that was it. No fire in the belly.

So, somebody was interested enough to try and buy a bit of peace and quiet. Not the first time that's ever happened in this business, and not the first time anyone's waved a C-note in front of my face. I'm pretty comfortable saying I've reached but never taken. It's not a case of scruples or being holier-than-thou, it's just the way I'm built. Makes life a little harder some days but I can sleep at night.

Cost me a dime and two cigarettes to find out the papers still had nothing at all on what happened the other night. I like my papers fresh, right off the bottom of the pile. Don't know if it's how they smell, or how they feel, but the kid on the corner knows that. He sees me coming he gets them ready, so I tip good. Doesn't mean the news is any better, but at least I'm not getting yesterdays with a fresh cover.

We've got two papers in this town, privately owned and

bitter rivals. They bird dog anyone and everyone, always on the lookout for that little extra something that's going to sell a few more pages or dig someone's grave a little deeper. Almost makes you feel sorry for the rich and famous, but it's their stupidity pays the bills.

Took a pew in a nearby park and skimmed through them both. Found nothing, which didn't surprise me, people died and disappeared in this fair city all the time. The fact that I had tripped over her made me think I'd interrupted someone else's disappearance, and he was trying to get that back on track. She was gone and there was no one to notice but me and him. He knew that, and the fact that I had her purse. That's one of the reasons why I'd gone to see ol' JG, they knew me so it only seemed fair I get to know them.

Thing about government paper is that it's hard to forge. They make it big and ugly for a reason. You can't get that kind of paper locally, which means somebody's uncle had a big fat contract to crank them out. And was probably none too careful, losing the odd sheet here and there that somebody else might pay a premium for. It was cheaper than relying on some weak-kneed civil servant to bypass the system. Most of them were too afraid of losing what was a cushy job for life to take any kind of a chance.

It was a safe bet I'd shaken JG up a little bit. His heart almost stopped when I'd showed my hand. His reaction told me he knew who it was for, but sure as hell wasn't going to spill it any time soon. Didn't surprise me but I'd given the tree a good shake. Something was bound to fall out sooner or later, and I was going to be there to catch whatever that was.

Figured I'd let him stew for a day or two and then go rattle his cage some more. That fat little weasel would probably wet his pants before giving up what I wanted to know, but he'd rather wet 'em than lose 'em. It was all about a good PI making something out of nothing, one step at a time.

Meantime I had other avenues to pursue. There had to be more to this, so while I waited for JG to run home crying to mama, I went looking for an old friend. He owed me from the last time I'd done something civic, and let him run a real barnburner of a story from an anonymous source. Sometimes airing out some dirty laundry could be more effective at proving innocence or guilt than a judge and jury.

My source was another eating machine, only Kelly was Irish and the heaviest drinker in the country bar none. Put even me to shame and I'd been known to wake up in some strange places. If nothing else he was a top-notch reporter, had a nose for news that would put a bloodhound to shame. Even knew about stuff that hadn't happened yet.

Kelly was the last one to argue that point. He slaved away, or so he would have you believe, for the better of the two papers. More often than not it was a case of him dictating to a copy boy five minutes before press time, leaving him plenty of time to drink the press bar dry and empty it of pickled eggs. The Irish are supposed to be the literary giants of the world but all Kelly could boast was a giant appetite for life, and a gut to prove it.

It was his nose for the big story that I admired most about him, if any part of a fat Irish slob was worth admiration. He could be halfway corked from a 12-hour lunch and still get to the scene of a murder-suicide faster than anyone else. And he knew pretty much everyone who was anyone in town. When he wasn't eating, belching, or dictating, he was on the telephone to somebody somewhere for details or a quote.

"So what've you heard lately," I asked, straddling the chair opposite him in the press bar.

"You? What are you doing here, I thought you were dead!" He was glad to see me.

"Good to see you, too, you big Irish lump."

"Now is that anyway to greet an old friend, especially one that's going to do you a favour?" He smiled knowingly, like he was JG's confessor and knew all.

"Really. And how would you know that. Can't a guy just drop in and say hi once in a while?" I asked.

"Friends, yes, you, no. You want something, you always do. What is it this time, and there had better be something good in it for me, or you can be off, you English heathen."

I smiled at that. We were always horse trading and today it was my turn for the horse.

"As it just so happens I do." And I gently fished out the big green Naturalisation document and passed it over to him.

"And this is?"

"A mystery."

"They always are with you,' he said, peering intently at it while he unfolded. "Ah, here we go. Number 18542 The Naturalisation Act Certificate of Naturalisation granted to a person, blah blah blah, very nice. What's this got to do with me?"

"Nothing to do with you. Got it off some stiff the other day, dead woman, no identification, all very mysterious, blah blah blah."

"I'm sure," he said in an unbelieving tone.

"You will note that it's blank."

"So I see, and just how did you accomplish that miracle, I wonder? These aren't just given away in a Crackerjacks box."

Two frosty mugs of foam magically appeared in the remains of Kelly's lunch. I slipped the barkeep a five. Kelly's eyebrows went up when he saw that.

"This must be important if you're spending that kind of money on humble little me."

"There's nothing humble about you, my friend, including your ego. So, what can you tell me about this, hear anything, ring any bells?"

He paused before answering, rubbing one of his many chins thoughtfully. Took a deep breath and shot down almost a full mug, carefully setting the remainder down on a cleaner part of the table. He steepled his fingers together and rested one of his chins on them, pretending to think deeply.

"Nothing factual, you understand, nothing that could stand up in court, just rumours, and things I see coming in on the wire."

"Okay, I'm listening." I sipped, both ears at the ready.

"Seems there's this rumour going around about foreign girls, Ukrainians, Poles, Russkies and the like, coming over here to work as private domestics, nannies, and the like. Maybe pick up a husband along the way. All very quiet, all very unofficial. They don't have money, don't speak English too good, and sure as hell don't have any papers. Who gets them over here I haven't heard, but the rumours are it's somebody local, possibly somebody new in town.”

"None of the local boys? And no one’s making a stink, that’s a new one. Usually they’re the first ones to complain, especially that nut Walton in the north end. Last I heard he’d stuffed someone down a manhole just for looking at his sister at church.”

"No stink, at least none that I know of. Mind you, they aren’t really all that bright any of them, with the possible exception of your old friend Panychkin. Him I could see being involved in this, but the rest of ‘em, bah!” He shot back the rest of his beer and sleeved his mouth clean.

Well, that narrowed it down to only one guy who wanted me dead. Panychkin always did have a high opinion of himself, what with his tailored suits and fancy cars. But I couldn’t see it, this wasn’t his style.

"And what makes you say that?” said Kelly.

"She was knifed, not something he prides himself on. He may be a lot of things, all of them bad, but if he wants you dead it’ll be a nine millimetre invitation.”

"Ah.”

"So, this rumour of yours got a name?”

"Nope, just telling you what I hear.”

"Yeah, well, try hearing a little harder would ya, I can’t shoot a rumour.”

I drained the last of my beer and got up to leave. Kelly gave me a disappointed look, like I’d taken his last pencil and him with a building on fire to report.

"Off so soon, why I’ve barely had time to insult you! Stay awhile, pull up another beer! Hey, barman, another round here and be quick about it!” He belched loudly enough to rattle the windows. The barkeep nodded and started pulling a couple.

"Sorry, maybe next time.” And with that I was off to see the one person who might be able to name Kelly’s rumour. She knew all about private domestics, the kind you don’t write home to momma about.

She was Sandy, a pert little redhead with legs down to here and a chest out to there and on the lookout for a husband. Trouble is she was only looking as far as me. Not exactly what you’d call an old flame but we'd known each other for quite awhile. Despite her occupation I had only ever come to her rescue once. It was dark, she was hurting, and he died ugly.

She and some other girls ran an independent flesh operation right downtown, in an area full of warehouses, ancient streets, and hungry men. There were a lot of others in the business, all of them tied to someone or some outfit for their protection, but not her. She'd survived all these years on her own, mainly by keeping a low profile and developing a small stable of reliable girls and wealthy men.

She was kinda my type, if there even was such a thing, but every so often she'd get sentimental and toss the words "settle down" and "honest woman" at me. Not that I was much of a catch but I kept hands off for two reasons. I sure as hell wasn't ready to be tied down to anyone or anything, and she knew things. She and the girls heard a lot of things down on the street that even I couldn't get wind of. Besides, I'd have to give up drinking and I haven't met a scotch yet that I didn't like.

She and several of the girls were sunning themselves on a couple of benches outside her front door. They were collectively showing more skin than a naked elephant, which was having an effect on traffic. I scooted over in between two Model T's tangled up in the median lane, both drivers taking their time about settling things.

Sandy untangled herself from the clothes she was half wearing and gave me a hug. I don't like people getting close to me, even if it's just for a hug. Bad things tend to happen to them and I didn't want to add her to the list.

"Well, hey, handsome, what brings you back to the land of the living," she grinned.

"Just the thought of your smiling face, honey. Just thought I'd drop in and say hi."

"Liar. What is it this time?" Now it was a pout.

"Nothing in particular. Just chasing down a rumour is all."

"Yeah, that's all it ever is with you, isn't it? Chasing something down." She paused for a second. "Something I gotta worry about?"

"Nah, just thought maybe you heard something, seen something last little while."

"Uh huh. Got a name?"

"No."

"Address, shoe size?"

"No."

"Geez, some detective you are! Look, I can't read minds so unless you got something else…"

We were wandering down the street, two old soldiers doing a little catching up. I lit up a pair of Luckies and passed her one. Two trails of smoke followed us down the block to a bench by a bus stop. She took a corner while I put a foot up and rested my smoking arm on it.

"That's just the problem, I don't. I got a stiff, female, no ID, and that's all."

CHAPTER FIVE

She grimaced. "Will you stop saying that? We aren't stiffs, in case you hadn't noticed."

"Yeah, well, you're still alive, she isn't, and that's the problem. Somebody got to her before I did and now I'm playing catch up."

"And that's it?"

"Yeah that's it. I was just hoping…"

"Hoping for what? A miracle, a sign from god? That doesn't happen in this town! Best I can do is ask around a little, but that might take a little time. You know my boys, they're a little gun-shy about certain things, especially if a badge is asking."

"Cops have badges, I got a license."

"That's not all you got. Geez, just look at you. What'd you do, sleep on the floor again? And gimme that jacket, there's a button missing."

"Yeah, it's been like that for a while. I just use the other ones."

"What other buttons, there aren't any. I swear you'd wander around naked if it wasn't for me."

"No worries there," I smirked, "although I could say much the same for you."

"Don't even think it, bucko. I'm in the business but not in the business, you know that."

"Yeah, a guy can always dream, can't he?" That brought a blush to her cheeks. The jacket landed in a heap beside her on the bench, my gun out in broad daylight for the first time in months.

"So, what are you hearing, or do I want to know?" I asked quietly.

She exploded. "It's always the same with you isn't it, you can't come around just to say hi? It's always gotta be so-and-so's dead or missing or lost and what do I know about it!" Not the reaction I was hoping for. Took a deep breath and kept on going.

"So, what is it, what have you heard?"

"Not as much as you think. Sometimes we just live to live and that's it."

"Yeah, well, I know you better than that. The whole reason you're here and not some fancy hole uptown is because of what you know, and who."

"And don't know, and won't say."

"Ah come on, if it'll make you feel any better I'll apologise but…" and that's as far as I got.

I heard the engine long before I saw the car but it didn't register until too late. No reason around here to accelerate unless you see a cop. And he wasn't all that much trouble. A nice guy with two kids, he got more whistles than the girls. They were like that, a man in uniform walks by and they give him the gears. What's a guy gonna do with a bunch of half-naked amazons razzing him. He learns to walk a little faster and smile a little harder.

A big black sedan tore around the corner on two wheels and screamed to a halt beside me. Two goons in dark suits poured out, guns drawn. I looked at Sandy, she gave me a look, and my hands went up. We three did the dance back to the car, climbed into the back, and tore away from the curb with a squeal of rubber. She watched in silence, holding on tight to my jacket.

The ride across town was quick, quiet, and uneventful. My two escorts, stone-faced and silent, sat me between them, thin meat in a very ugly sandwich. Didn't recognise either one but then I'm not exactly on a first name basis with every hood in town. A lot of ugly comes my way but it's usually pretty angry and out to do some nasty. And you wonder why I shoot first.

These two were almost civilised the way they helped themselves to my piece and my smokes. No knuckles across the chin, no knife in the ribs, just a quick pat down and we were off and running. So, who was it that wanted me alive and kicking, I wondered. Most rides like this started in the trunk and ended with a kicking, delivered down a dark alley or in an empty lot. Not something I was looking forward to.

Some twenty minutes later we pulled up at the back of a three-storey apartment block in the more upscale part of town. This neighbourhood flaunted success like a Broadway musical on opening night. The doormen sniffed loudly at guys like me, and hustled us in through side doors like we were last week's laundry.

Charming.

Money talked pretty loudly in this town, and while it could buy a lot of things, silence wasn't always one of them. Dirty laundry wasn't anything new, but those who could afford it paid extra for the silence service. It wasn't my place to pass judgement, I just did whatever needed doing and vanished quietly into the night. Who better to hire than someone who knew his way around dirt and could be quick and quiet.

Some sweet young thing gets it into her head he's serious, when all he wants is something warm to call when he's bored, and then send home with the milkman. That's usually where I came in, no rough stuff, just a hand with the packing, and a ticket out of town. They don't always go quietly but they do go.

We took the stairs two at a time, my armpits substituting for my feet. It was a fast but painful way to travel. We arrived at the penthouse in double quick time, my shoes leaving skid marks on the parquet. Might have been a nice view but I was too busy flying through some open French doors to notice.

Seems we'd arrived a little early, no one came to check my coat or help me up. Or check for an ankle piece. My old pal from Texas wasn't the only one packing a little extra in his pants. Got mine off a guy trying to lift my wallet while I was crawling home one night after a really good poker game. I might have been half corked but I didn't like strangers putting their mitts on me. I broke the one holding the gun.

Shook off the dust and went to work, nosing around to see what I could see.

Seems this guy had money to burn, judging by the price tags still attached to the furniture. Everything looked new, right down to the paint on the walls. Wonderful. Somebody new in town with cash in hand was never good news. I already had my hands full with the regulars.

Found the sideboard and poured myself a Scotch, three fingers, no ice. I wandered around, looking for smokes and trying not to chug my glass. This wasn't scotch it was liquid heaven, silky smooth going down, a gentle aftertaste, and a slow fire in the belly that just begged you to keep the fires stoked. Whoever he was the man had taste, I had to give him that. A strong male voice, slightly accented, interrupted my appreciation of the quality of his hooch.

"Mr Ford, I presume?" The voice wandered into the room from behind me.

"Yeah, that's right. Nice place you got here," I replied, turning around slowly. "New in town?"

"Thank you, and yes, I am. The name is Constantine, Peter Constantine."

Shifted my drink left and shot out my right. "Hey, Pete, pleased to me you. Tony, Tony Ford!" He shook it limply with a soft, well-manicured hand.

"You seem to be doing pretty good. Insurance? Real estate?" I took another sip and looked him over from tip to toe. Smallish, medium complexion, thinning hair, wire-framed glasses, studious looking. Add a tailored suit, spit-shined brogans and a silk tie and you had the picture of man full of himself. And all of it nasty.

He smiled faintly, as if I'd picked up on some kind of inside joke. He didn't strike me as the joking kind.

"A little bit of this and a little bit of that, and yes, some real estate, but no, no insurance. I do however have a modest interest in people."

"Same here. I'm a PI, what's your angle?"

"Call it human relations, if you will." He sauntered over to the sideboard and poured himself a drink, single finger of the same scotch with lots of ice. Something to sip, and not to drink, which made him a thinker, the most dangerous kind of nasty. He wanted to keep a clear head for whatever was to come. And that wasn't going to be good for me.

"Really, so what kind of relations we talking about."

He paused a second, and took a sip. "People these days, it's such a troubled world, have a need to get from here to there, quietly, without all the interest certain other people might express. Official interest, you understand. Difficult if you don't have documents, and even more so if you don't speak the language or have any money."

"Yeah, I can see where that might be a problem. So why you?"

"All I do is that which my parents did for me," he said,

smiling faintly, "help people along a little, ease a few restrictions, and so on."

"That's very noble of you."

"Thank you. I do what little I can."

"Pays well does it, helping all those people going from here to there? I don't suppose a guy like you does it for free."

He smiled evilly. "It has its moments, yes. Being a private investigator you must have many of your own, correct?"

"Yeah, like the one I had the other night. There I am down a dark alley, all on my lonesome, when I trip over some stiff in an alley. Took a look around, asked a couple of questions, and here I am. Funny how that works."

"And here you are. What was it about her that caught your attention so?" he asked quietly. His eyes never left mine.

"Oh, I don't know, sometimes it's just the little things. I'm not much of a big picture guy. All I know is what I see around me. Like stabbed instead of shot, well dressed and all alone and no money for a cab. Makes me wonder…"

"Did you ascertain if she had a name, where she was from?"

"Wasn't very talkative at the time. That's how it is when you're dead."

"Ah, I see. How unfortunate for her." Did I detect a hint of a smile?

"Yeah, there's a lot of that going around right now."

"And so here you are making inquiries, how very kind of you. But really not necessary, I assure you. Isn't that what we pay the police for? Perhaps if you allowed them to do their job, you could do what private detectives do, whatever that is, and not waste your time with this particular inquiry."

I took a deep breath before I replied. "Can't do that. I'm kinda on the clock."

"Really?" he asked, surprised. "And who might have hired you, if I may ask."

"You can ask but I can't tell," I said. "Client confidentiality. It's a PI thing."

"I see," he said, sounding unhappier by the second.

"So, let me ask you," I said, smiling broadly. "I get a free cab ride and a couple of drinks, you must want something in return. What might that be I wonder. Little help with the paperwork, maybe? Tell the truth I can't write worth a damn but I know a couple of good secretaries."

He shot me a look that would have stunned an elephant. "What I want is for you to stay out of my business," he growled.

"Still haven't said what that is, exactly."

"Like I said, Mister Ford."

"Tony, to my friends."

"As I was saying…. Tony."

"But you ain't one of them."

There was silence for few moments while he digested this bit of news. I waited for my travelling companions to return. Since the booze wasn't loosening my tongue I figured they were going to show up any minute and get in a little more exercise, with their fists. I waited, nervous as hell, sipping the last of my anaesthesia.

"As I was saying, I deal with people. They come to me with certain needs and I help them fulfil those needs. Those needs do not include murder inquiries from the likes of you. It upsets them, and me."

"Must be hard to do when they turn up dead. How much they pay you for this service of yours. Must be plenty for guy like you to rent out a place like this."

"Without a name I'm afraid I can't help you, or whomever it is you might be working for."

"That's me all over, doing what I'm good at, being a nosey pain in the ass PI. Got any more of this?" I asked waving my empty glass.

He scowled. Maybe he was mad that I was taking advantage of the free drink offer. Giving away six fingers of the good stuff doesn't always sit well with people. Especially when their guests choke it down in one shot and go looking look for more. This was supposed to be accompanied by a good cigar and loose company but I didn't see any lying around.

"No," he growled darkly.

"That's too bad, I was starting to like you." Gave him a big goofy grin in return.

"The feeling is not mutual, I assure you."

"Didn't think it was," I quipped, helping myself to another three fingers. They went down in a single fiery gulp. Felt good but sure as hell made the eyes water. Quality stuff.

"But I must insist you leave such things alone. Understand that your nose doesn't belong here."

"I'm a little old to be going back to school, Pete. You don't mind me calling you Pete, do you? Try telling me what to do again and see where it gets you." I didn't like threats, especially from penny ante thugs like him. Us two dogs were pulling on the same bone and he was losing.

He carefully put his glass back down on a table beside the couch and snapped his fingers sharply. My two friends reappeared. He nodded in my direction and took up where they'd left off. I gave Petey my best I don't give a damn smile as they lifted me up off me feet. He lit a cigarette in reply, blowing the smoke my way.

"Take my advice Mr Frances, and leave this particular … problem ... alone. Your reputation precedes you, which is why I am giving you the courtesy of a warning, before any further harm might befall you. I am sure there are many other people in similar difficulties who might benefit from your expertise. She is not one of them. Leave her alone, as I will you. Otherwise we shall meet again…under less friendly circumstances, I assure you."

I grinned wickedly at him as I was being dragged away. "Thanks for the drinks Pete, nice meeting you. Oh, wait, there is one more thing I forgot to mention, something you might like to know."

"And what might that be," he growled.

"I never said it was a she, you did."

Sandy was right where I'd left her, holding up a wall and filing a nail. Trudy, a big brunette, was stretched out along the bus bench in front, idly sunning herself. Neither one of them seemed to notice that I'd been gone, like my being snatched off the street in broad daylight was a regular thing. Didn't even bat an eye when I returned the way I'd left, heaved out the door along with my piece and an empty pack of smokes. Laid out flat on the sidewalk and that was that, an hour out of my day filled with a year's worth of curiosity.

Sandy sauntered over to the corpse, helped me stand up, and walked me back inside like I was her grandfather. I sure as hell felt like one, kissing cement will do that to a guy. Trudy yawned loudly as we passed, stretching those gorgeous gams of hers halfway to China, examining her toes with exaggerated interest. Blew me a kiss and went back to sunning herself.

Joy girls, working girls, call them what you will, that side of life was full to overflowing with warm hearts and warmer bodies, and plenty of takers. Holier-than-thous and political wannabes were always beating the drum of morality and trying to move them along. They were easy targets and took more than their fair share of political purity. Once elected however, it was almost a rite of passage for them to tour the dark side, get a first-hand feel for things, so to speak.

Sandy's place was right downtown, one of the few houses left in a neighbourhood full of old buildings and older dreams. Insurance or taxes had claimed most of them, leaving the neighbourhood empty of life. It was the same old story all over town, only made harder by the times. You owed you paid, period, and if you couldn't the bailiffs would take what was left, along with your dignity and your soul. Kicking down doors for them was a small, but financially necessary, part of my business. They sure as hell paid me, which allowed me to keep my soul, if not my dignity.

Her main floor front was one large parlour, which allowed for any number of visitors at a time, backed by a private dining room and kitchen. The upstairs was all business, the girls living out of their rooms and sharing everyone and everything. Except me.

I was hands off, not because I wanted to be but because someone else did. I got that, even though she knew I wasn't exactly the marrying kind. The PI business was dangerous enough without some hot-tempered housewife wondering where the hell you'd been tonight. There was nothing special here, just shoe leather and a gun, with no ambition beyond seeing the sun rise every morning. Didn't have a mother growing up, and sure as hell didn't want one now.

Hers wasn't the nicest life either but it struck me as the more human. Here was a place where money bought a kind of happiness that seemed to pass by most of us, even those claiming to be happily married. Didn't know why that was but the joint was always jumping. I didn't fault Sandy and the girls for what they did, you go where the money is, just like me.

The interior was cool and quiet, more like a cheap hotel with all its cheesy décor than what it really was. I'd been inside a few times, on business, but I could never get over the collection of crap that surrounded me. In a place that ran through more people than the bus stop out front, the girls sure as hell didn't spend their leisure hours painting their toes.

Every corner, shelf, bookcase and square inch of floor was jammed with little statue things. Thousands of them, in every shape and size possible. Horses, pigs, and cows side by side with trees, buildings, and god knows what else. Figurines the girls called them, statuettes, and aren't they just the cutest things. They came from all over the world supposedly, some of them supplied by their customers, but most picked up by the girls on their day off.

Claudette was the ringleader, a red-haired dynamo straight off the farm. She literally got off the bus right out front one day, broke and crying, with her whole life in two bags. Sandy took her in, dried her tears, gave her a room. In return, she got the hardest working girl on the face of the planet, and a building full of things that required as much care and attention as her customers. She doesn't work upstairs, she's too nice a kid Sandy confided, but she's got the girls organised just like the army.

"Could be worse," said Sandy, as she slid a cold beer across the kitchen table. "With business going as good as it is, they don't have much time off anyways. And what time they do get off she's got them cleaning and polishing the things. It's like living in a damn china shop."

"Helluva shop."

"No kidding. And the real crazy thing is they keep the place spotless. Not just the statue things but the whole damn place! I'm afraid to sneeze in case I mess something up. It's like my gramma's living room used to be."

I knew the feeling, my old bible-spouting gran was much the same way. She never made me eat off the floor but I could sure see my face in it.

A couple of pulls and Sandy started calling for my jacket. The mother in her just wouldn't let it go. Her man, coatless in her kitchen, no way. Ironic considering that any other man in her place would be minus more than just his coat. Moments later it appeared in the doorway, courtesy of a lean white hand tipped with red nail polish.

I slid it on, noting how it didn't smell anymore and wasn't stained with anything. And all the buttons worked, which Sandy showed me with some pride, brushing out some invisible creases. Cigarette smoke lazily drifted in from next door, reminding me that mine were long gone. Sandy took the hint and lit a pair. I took one gratefully, ignoring the red lipstick that came with it.

"That's Lena, she's new," she said nodding her head towards the raven-haired dressing gown seated at the dining room table. It was covered with my stuff, papers all neatly unfolded and flattened out, several pieces of jewellery set out in a neat row to one side. I thought I'd given it all to Fatman, must have missed a pocket somewhere.

"I know better than to ask where it came from, but Lena thinks she might know who it belongs to, ain't that right honey?"

"Really?"

"Yeah, really. Lena's from the old country, reads a lot of things, speaks a bunch of different languages and stuff. You can read all that stuff, right honey?"

A pair of soulful dark lidded eyes looked up at me. "Yes, I read many things. I read this."

We wandered into the dining room. Sandy pulled out a chair and shoved me into it. "Sorry about the mess. The girls had to empty your pockets to get this…thing… clean. Lena saw the papers and started reading. Next thing you know …well, she'll tell you."

Lena was hunched over the dining table, resting on her elbows like a gypsy woman reading a fortune, mine. She did me a favour and fingered the old country stuff first. In deep, mournful whispers, she told me enough about my client to keep me quiet as a mouse for two cigarettes.

"Certificate of baptism which is this", she said pointing to a ratty piece of paper. "Her name is Adelaida Natalia Lenovskaya."

Adelaida was born and baptised into the Greek Catholic Church in some backwater south of nowhere Austria in the year of our Lord 1898, month of March, the 21st day. Which would make her close to forty something. So, why were you here I wondered. Why come all this way just to die in an alley?

"This is from my church," said Lena, pointing to a raffle ticket. "I go there every Sunday morning, I say prayers. I say one for her too, now." And maybe I'll ask the good father, did she confess something I should know about. I didn't have a problem leaning on a collar now and again. In this business information is where you find it. Besides, the big guy had more important souls to save, this one wasn't worth the effort.

The lecture continued. I asked the obvious and got a soulful look in return, which roughly translated meant yes, you idiot man, this is her whole life. There was part of a letter from sister to brother, apparently brother Walter had a new son, and the baptism was set for a date and place on a missing page. Some faded photographs, one of a group of men leaning on a tractor, another of somebody's kid leaning out of a cart on a farm somewhere. A small record book of payments to a Relief Association dated from last year, not from around here. All very nice but of no use to me, I couldn't exactly go to her home town and knock on doors.

It was looking more and more like the papers were hers, but why hadn't she signed it any of it. She wasn't rich, I knew that, she had connections enough to make it here and try for a new start in life. The why of it was the mystery but then what would my life be without one. Only problem was my client was dead, and the somebody who might know the answers had already warned me off. This was getting better and better.

I waved my empty bottle at Sandy and she shot me a look.

"This also I have," Lena said indicating the blank naturalisation form. "I … need one when I come here, stay for Sandra."

"Mind my askin' who you got it from?"

"Yes. I not tell."

"Does the name Peter Constantine mean anything to anybody," I asked innocently.

It suddenly got very cold in the room. Sandy's grip on my shoulder tightened enough to make me wince.

"Why do you want to know," she hissed. I gently removed the claw and rotated my shoulder back to life.

"Just a name I came across, you know how it is. Things come up, I gotta ask."

"Let me guess. Your little field trip have anything to do with it?"

"Could be."

Sandy began to pace around the room, arms tightly folded across her chest, lips drawn tight. She was more intense than I'd seen in some time. Lena sat straight up in her chair, stone-faced and silent.

"Wanna tell me about it. If it means something, I gotta know, doll."

"Not much to tell," she growled. "Bastard came to see me last month, told me, TOLD ME, I needed him and his protection, otherwise things would happen. Unpleasant things as he put it, to me and the girls."

Now she was waving her arms around like she was conducting an orchestra.

"I have to work for him, pay him fifty percent, and take in a couple new girls every so often. New girls! Like the old ones aren't good enough!"

That got my attention. Now I was sitting straight up, stone faced but definitely not silent. "He was here?"

"Yeah, but I told him no, I…"

"Wait, wait, wait," I growled, half rising out of my seat. "He was here, that smarmy bastard was here? And he threatened you?"

"It's not as bad as it sounds."

"I don't care how it sounds, a dame is dead because of him and you're not going to be next," I growled.

"Relax big man, this isn't your fight, it's mine I can handle him!" snapped Sandy.

Now I was on my feet, more than ready to shoot something, or someone. I'd been playing this far too loose and let it get too close to home, and now there were others involved that shouldn't be.

There was a danger here that I had been too quick to dismiss, or was it that I was so used to it that I was ignoring it. Either way this was my doing, and I was going to deal with it. Pronto.

"No, you can't, not this guy. I've seen his work and it's not pretty, just ask her." I said pointing to the papers on the table. "This is my fight, not yours. Stay out of it, I'll deal with him."

"No, leave it alone, please. I know you, you'll go off half-cocked and shoot him full of holes and I don't want that on my conscience," she pleaded. She looked like she was about to cry.

"Conscience, nothing, you shoulda told me! I could have done something about it! Warn him off maybe, or something…." The words were deep and dark, coming from that place I didn't like going to.

"You don't need to worry about me, I'll, we'll, be okay, really." Sandy spoke softly, staring shyly at a very angry me, looking a little flushed. She knew she'd just lit the fuse on a very large stick of dynamite. Question was, could she stop it before it went off?

"Yeah, well I worry, alright, about you, about Lena here, about this whole damn place! So sue me!" The words shot out of my mouth like shells from a Thompson, hard and fast.

Next thing I know she's sprinted across the room and grabbed me in a bear hug. I didn't know where to put my hands so I held them up like I was about to give in to something.

"Hey, hey, easy on the suit, sister, I just got it cleaned."

"Oh, you great big beautiful man, you I always knew you had a heart in there somewhere," she murmured, face buried deep in my lapels.

"Yeah, well, don't get your hopes up, I'm just saying is all. Now lemme go do my job."

"I know," she said, taking a step back, brushing her tears off my suit. "I know, and that's what counts, right?"

"If you say so. Look, Sandy, just promise me one thing, okay?"

"What's that?"

"If he comes sniffing around here again, you call me, day or night, I wanna know, okay? We'll have a little talk, me and him, set things straight."

"Promise, just don't do anything stupid. I kinda like having you around." And with that the she broke free, cuffed back more tears, and took a deep breath. "Okay, now sit down and let's get back to work, I gotta open up soon."

I sat.

"Now, what did he say about the new girls, where they were from, anything like that?"

"No, just that they would be new, and might need a little help getting started. If I helped him he'd cut me a deal to forty percent."

"I know where," said Lena softly, "I know where from." We both stared at her.

"What, how?" gasped Sandy.

"This man, this Constantine, he come in big car, yes, with man to drive car. I hear them, they speak Russian, I hear what they say. They are from old country, I go ask driver man in car, ask him where, maybe I know from where."

"And what did he say, honey," whispered Sandy.

She sat back in her chair, sighing heavily. "They are from old country, my country, Russia. He come here with this man Constantine, work for him. Protect him, protect his business."

"Again, what about the girls?" I asked.

"There is much trouble there. They want to come here but they have no money, no papers, no place. That one would give this all to them, but they have to give him everything in return, work for him, maybe as a Night Butterfly."

"A what?"

"Night butterfly. What I do. What we all do here."

"Oh." Just when I thought I'd heard it all.

Now it was Lena's turn to lighten the mood, large Russian tears slowly dribbling down her cheeks. Sandy moved to put her arms around Lena's shoulders, whispering quietly into her ear. Lena sniffled loudly and nodded, sleeving the waterfalls off her face and whispering back.

Everybody was upset, I got that. Petey had more coming to him than he knew, but I was burning daylight sitting here. Sandy looked up at me, all soulful and sad, which I figured was my cue to finish the lecture and get what I could out of Lena. Did she know how, did she know who, did she ... Sandy grabbed my left ear and dragged me out of the room.

"What the hell do you think you're doing?" she growled.

"My job," I growled back, massaging some life back into my lobe. "I got a stiff with no name and an itch named Peter I'm dying to scratch. So what am I supposed to do, learn Russian? I gotta know things and she's all I got."

"Well not right now, okay. Poor girl has suffered enough. Let me talk to her a little later and I'll see what I can find out. Meantime you shoo … go on … shoo." And with a determined shove sent me on way. So I shooed and took a stroll to nowhere.

I'm no saint, I don't pretend to be one, I just do a job that gets me shot at more than most. I drink too much, don't charge enough, can't always remember where I was the night before, and have a habit of taking on cases that a dead dog wouldn't sniff at. And, as Sandy so helpfully pointed out, I can be a little too quick to pass on the real work of the day. Sometimes you just want to get out there and shoot something. Like now.

Chance or fate or karma or whatever had dumped this woman into my lap, and then twisted the knife by adding Sandy and the girls to the mix. True, I'd taken up their cause some time ago, but I'd gotten a little lazy and failed them all. One was dead and the rest were under the gun and it was all on me. There was this pit in my stomach that guilt was digging and I didn't like how deep it was going.

CHAPTER SIX

I ate up the pavement like I was trying to make Tipperary by nightfall, smoking like a chimney, anger trying to get past my smarter self just long enough to make me do something stupid. Caring was a dirty word in this business, a word that held more distractions than a shapely leg, and more danger than a fully loaded Thompson. So, was that why I was tearing through the downtown, gun in my hand, a round chambered? Maybe.

As tempting as it was to track Constantine down and let some anger out, my smarter self passed on the notion after a couple blocks of hard charging, and harder breathing. Pulling the trigger on him might feel good and ease up on the guilt some, but it would leave too many questions unanswered. There had to be more to it than this, more lost souls like my client wandering along the road to the promised land. It was too bad Constantine was their tour guide but maybe I could still do something about that. There was no saving this lost soul but no reason why theirs couldn't be.

Fine, I gasped to myself, grabbing at a lamppost for support, you win this round. But just remember my friend, tomorrow is another day. Round two is going to be on me.

Funny thing about your smarter self, you do your best to lock it up like a crazed relative with a death wish and a live grenade, but it still manages to do its best to steer you onto the straight and narrow. Mine wasn't that brave, but it knew me well enough to throw me into a red leather booth and tell me to sit still. Who was I to argue?

I was barely through my first cigarette when a plateful of hot and greasy appeared in front of my nose. It slammed onto the table, barely dodging the cutlery that came with it.

"So what's this?"

"Dinner. Eat."

"Do I have to? I'm still kinda full from breakfast."

The hand that had delivered the plate slowly sat down across from me, along with its owner. I pretended not to notice and dug in. Stella was in one of her rare good moods, which meant she wanted something. Nothing ever came without a price in her world so I chewed fast and waited for the other shoe to drop.

Making like a hungry vulture on a stakeout, she watched every bite with those beady little eyes of hers. It wasn't like I was going to steal the china or anything, but giving up a free meal pained her. Or was it the fact that I was the one getting it?

"So whadda you want," I asked in between gulps. "I know this is breaking your heart so what gives."

"Getting up a little game tonight, last minute thing, 7th and Main, number five. You know the place, right?"

"Yeah I know it. So who's playing, anybody I need to worry about?"

"Not this time, they're all regulars, guys you've met before including those city swanks, Mungo and Parker. I owe them one for what happened last time so they're sitting in for free."

"Fair enough."

"Listen, I got that new kid, what's-his-name…uh…you know…"

"Yeah, I know who you mean."

"He's sitting in tonight but it's his first time with a big table. How 'bout you go on over and sit with him. Half stakes okay?"

And there it was, she needed me to ride herd on another newbie, probably a cousin or other needing a job. Not that it was difficult, just more of a pain in the ass. It was hard enough keeping track of everything without anything stronger than coffee to help pass the time. Junior had to learn how to deal the right way, not off the bottom too much, and not bet the farm on a pair of twos. Playing sober was like pulling teeth with rusty pliers, torture. I groaned loudly.

"And don't shoot anybody this time, okay?"

"Yeah okay fine."

Dawn came up more quietly this time around. Everybody played like gentlemen, cashed out quietly and went home with the milkman, leaving me with nothing to do but yawn and stretch. One look from me and the kid was on his knees scrubbing the floor. I stepped over to the window and lit my tenth cigarette of the day in salute to the sunrise. Stella was going to be in a good mood when I gave her the take for the night, and so she was. So much so that she actually patted me on the back and thanked me. Life was just full of surprises.

Me, I hadn't felt this good in a long time. I was relatively sober, full to brim with Stella's love and affection, and a wad of her cash was burning a hole in my pocket. Could life be any sweeter? Probably not, but then who was I to question life's decisions. Usually it threw road apples at me and stomped all over me for good measure. But not today. I had it in mind to do what I enjoy best on a day like today and do a little hurtin', and I knew just he guy to do it to.

Now was as good a time as any to start scratching that itch a little and revisit my old pal Vance. I couldn't be sure he was working for Constantine but the odds were pretty good. That schmuck had to know more than he was saying, but he wasn't about to sing it from the rooftops. It was going to require some personal attention on my part, and I can't say as I wasn't looking forward to it. I'm old school. I like to get up close and personal when I interview somebody, look them right in the eye when I ask the questions they can't, or won't, answer. What follows isn't pretty but I get what I want.

And if that wasn't enough I made an offhand remark about Vance to Stella, and got another surprise in return.

"He's definitely not like that," she spat. "You'll have to shoot him in the balls first, if you can find them. Bastard's a real prick."

"I take it you've met him before."

"Yeah. Got into a little legal trouble couple years back." She took a deep breath. "Remember that fancy pants you caught cheating and kicked his ass out for me? I never told ya but he came back with some hard ass lawyer and tried to get me shut down. Had the boys from Health down and everything."

"You never said nothin' to me about it," I grumbled darkly.

"Yeah I know and I woulda, except it got so's I had to make a phone call or two … you know … couple days later he calls up all nice as pie and its over."

"And I take it Vance was the lawyer."

"Yeah. Bastard! He came this close to shutting me down," she groused, rubbing her thumb and index fingers together. "Say hi for me, will ya?"

I smiled grimly. "Oh yeah I'll say hi alright, for all of us."

Now I figured that good ol' JG was like every other suit in town, looking out for nobody but himself. He put his pants on one leg at a time, worked a solid eight hours a day fleecing widows and orphans, and ate lunch away from the office. In other words, a creature of habit, and judging by how well he filled out his chair, doing very well at it. It took me less than an hour to track down his favourite lunch spot, a little hole in the wall just two blocks over.

"Oh yes, he come here all the time," said the owner, staring hard at the left side of my suit coat. "Come every day, get Magda serve him, she big girl and he like dat. He always have soup and ham sandwich, he no like kielbassa. Not even my wife pyrogy, and she make so good."

"So, what time does all this gaiety and merriment take place?"

"Eh?"

"What time does he come here? When does he eat?"

"Oh yes, he come, uh, every day noon for sure. Church at corner rings bell for noon mass. Many people come then. I keep chair for him he like. He always pay cash money." He was going to pay something else today.

Time flies when you're having fun, or killing time until that special someone makes an appearance. I can hit the centre of a sewer grate with a butt from ten feet, I know what streetcars pass what corners at what time, and on average how many dames wear their skirts above the knee. And it never fails that the second you go off for more smokes or a mickey of something to stay awake with, something happens.

But not today, the second I took up my post that special something waddled out his front door, turned right, and strolled down the alley to find Magda and her twins. I'm sure he had evil thoughts on that score, but not as evil as the one that grabbed him by the shoulder halfway down the alley and spun him around. He went white as a sheet when he saw who the hand on his shoulder belonged to. Shoved him up against a wall and stepped back so he could get a good look. I had all the time in the world, and I wanted him to know it.

"Hello Vance, going somewhere? Lunch maybe, Magda sends her regards. How about we put that time to better use. There's a couple things we gotta talk over, you and me, stuff I didn't want to talk about in the office. Walls have ears, so I figured this might as good a place any."

"What do you want?" he whimpered. "I don't know anything. Honest, I don't."

"Really? That's not how I see it. Your eyes lit up like roman candles when I showed you all that paper the other day. I got a couple questions is all. Pony up and you'll be in time for dessert. Its pie I think. Apple"

"What paper, I don't know anything about any paper." He was shaking like a leaf in a hurricane. I smiled.

"Yeah you do, so enlighten me. Who do they belong to, where'd they come from."

"I don't know anything about that, I … uh … I can't say."

"Yeah, you can," I growled, grabbing him by his lapels and shoving my smiling face into his. "That's federal paper I've got, and you know it because you gave it to her, didn't you! It's blank, and possessing that's an even bigger mistake. Smart guy like you should know that, or didn't Constantine mention the twenty years that goes with getting caught with it."

I pushed off on him, and lit up a Lucky, snicking the match off the brick beside his left ear. Blew smoke at him while he gathered what was left of his thoughts.

"Look …uh … you seem like a reasonable fellow," he wheedled, swallowing hard. "Maybe I was just a little hasty during our earlier meeting. Perhaps if you could tell me what it is you're looking for I could help you."

A solid right to his gut drove any dreams of a quiet afternoon right out his mind, along with most of the air in his lungs. He leaned forward, hands on knees, gasping and wheezing like my gran used to after one of her bouts. Miner's lung she said, just like your grampa, only he'd never been near a mine his whole life. The docs said it might have been TB but she died before anyone could figure it out. That was one day I would never forget. I was hoping he would do the same.

I stood him up, grabbed his lapels, and started talking to him nose to nose. "Talk to me, fat boy. I wanna know what the hell is going on. Who are those papers for, where you'd get them from! And more importantly, who was she."

"Who was who?" He gasped. I slugged him again and he fell to his knees, barely able to breath.

"The dame in the alley, who was she!" I grabbed a handful of greasy hair and stood him back up to meet his maker. "The one you left to die."

"I don't know anything about that," he gasped, still struggling to breathe. "All she was supposed to do was …"

There was a squeal of tires and a car roared into the alley off to my left. A black coupe with a long hood and four big lights, a LaSalle maybe. It slowed down just as it came up to us, and a gun popped out the passenger side window and staring firing. The deep booms of a .45 came in regular succession, chipping a line along the brickwork before crossing JG's chest. Not the spray of a tommy gun but the deliberate aim of someone with a target in mind.

I was down in the dirt even as the first brick took a hit. I gave fire as the Coupe passed, leaving a line of holes along the side and rear. I didn't get a good look at the shooter it happened so fast, but I emptied a clip at them. There was a thud behind me, and then a spray of gravel as the Coupe sped up and shot out the other end of the alley and vanished.

I got up slowly, holstered my piece, and looked around but there were no other surprises coming. This had taken only a couple seconds but that had been enough. JG was sitting on the ground, his back to the brick wall, with a look of complete surprise on his face. I checked for a pulse but he was too dead to need one. So why him and not me I wondered. He hadn't spilled anything interesting, but somebody wanted to make sure he couldn't.

I fished out his wallet, found some cigars in a fancy silver case, and not much else. They were too thin to be Cuban but looked a decent smoke. His wallet was bulging with cash, he could drive, had a bank account downtown, and lived royally, judging by the address on his cheques. Taking the cash and the cigars I tossed everything else aside. Figured the alley wolves would find him before anybody else and help themselves. Not the nicest way to go but then what did guys like him really deserve.

A shrill whistle broke the calm, a flatfoot blowing reveille as hard as he could. He was inviting the whole world to the party I was hosting in the alley. That's all I didn't need. Badges and guns were a bad a mix in this town and my bail was getting too expensive. One last look at my latest problem and I was hotfooting it down the alley, and onto the nearest streetcar going anywhere. I stuffed a bill into the driver's pocket, walked quickly to the back and hunkered down.

Got off four blocks later, whistled up a cab and took a quicker and quieter ride back to the office. I was pretty sure I'd gotten away clean but now I had two bodies to deal with. Somebody official somewhere was bound to take note and that wasn't going to do me any good.

Great, just great, two bodies on my hands, and probably every flatfoot in town looking for me. Not exactly the first time I'd been wanted by half a city, but a reasonable explanation or cash probably wasn't going to cut it this time. You had to figure whoever set up the hit in the alley was already on the horn to the nearest station. *Officer, Officer, I saw the whole thing! It was that schmuck Ford. Gunned him down like a mad dog!* That somebody didn't like me in this burned-out burg was nothing new, it was just gonna make things a little difficult for a while.

I sucked back half a cigar trying to figure the angle on this. The ambush in the alley had been a neat enough trick. By rights I should've been downtown with some badge shining a light in my eyes and demanding to know my middle name. For the record, I don't have one. Gran always called me Anthony, which got me beat up a lot, until I grew up enough to beat the crap out of them. Then it was sir. The boys overseas called me Tone, everybody else just knew me as more trouble than I was worth.

I couldn't tell if it was me they were after or what I had in my pockets, but this sure as hell was becoming one big ruckus. Seems I was carrying the only breadcrumbs in town and every time I pulled them out things only got worse. They were leaving a trail a blind man could follow, and he was practically standing on my heels he was so close.

Now, I've seen enough dusters to know that the best way to break up a trail is to scuff up the dirt and rub out the tracks. Even the smartest rider can't follow up on that. It's hard to scuff up cement but I figured if the breadcrumbs disappeared, same thing. The trail dies and maybe I can put a little distance between me and the blind man.

He sure had a lot of friends, my blind compadre. Seemed like every corner in town had some poor sap with his hand out hoping for a smile, or a penny or two. Funny thing was they only showed between nine and five, and only downtown. Any other time you could have your pick of the litter down at Salvatore's, a dive pretending to be a greasy spoon and not doing too good at it. Place was jammed daily with the halt, the blind, and the lame, all drunk as skunks and grabbing every bottom that went by.

For the record, they were known as Sal's Army, and they lived by the motto, if you can't earn an honest living, then any living will do. They had the pity racket all sewn up, and were taking this town for more money than a crooked politician. And just like our elected bandits, they didn't take kindly to competition. Beatings were commonplace, with the real needy being tossed behind bars or escorted out of town, for their own good.

I didn't think Constantine had dragged them into this but I put the eyes in the back of my head to work. I only had so much ammunition, and only one nerve left, so the next person to cough had better duck first. I stopped in at the office just long enough to catch my breath and start scuffing the dirt.

The trail of breadcrumbs vanished with the help of a couple of loose floorboards, the result of a long night of liquid research. You try to pull an all-nighter on a divorce case and wake up with part of the floor in your hands. To this day I can't remember how that little discovery came to be, but it turned out to be better than a bank. And there was no combination to remember.

There was just enough room under those boards for things that might have meant something to somebody, only they were dead. Not that I'm sentimental, but some of them might raise more questions than answers if they ever saw the light of day. I deposited my latest problems within, pulled my last two clips of ammo, and that was that.

Then I was off and running again, my fingertips were itching like crazy. You know that itch, the one that says run don't walk to the nearest exit, and don't look back? Yeah, that one, so I hit the road, heading for who knows where, and ran smack dab into two uniforms strolling along like they owned the place. They were all smiles and apologies for bumping into an honest and decent citizen like me, until one of them spotted my underarm protection.

"Hey," said the eagle-eyed one, slowly dusting himself off. "You gotta piece there I see. You got a license for that? Hey, Charlie, he's gotta…." And that was it. The hands that were slowly reaching for the sky shoved them both backwards, hard, into a couple of dames who had stopped to watch the action. Purses and curses mixed it up like a night at the fights.

I tore out of there like my tail was on fire, up a street, down an alley, and gone. Which, to tell the truth, wasn't all that far. A couple of blocks and my lungs were screaming for mercy. Two chases in one day, it felt worse than being shot. I staggered into an alcove, looking for something, anything to park my lungs on, praying that the uniforms had given up. All I found was Ronald Colman.

His ugly mug was plastered all over a movie poster, along with some woman I didn't recognise, doing something shady with two flags. At first I thought it was some kind of recruiting poster, until a voice like a gravel truck rumbled in my ear.

"Hey there handsome, wanna buy a ticket? Twenty-five cents gets you the front row."

The truck was sitting in a glass telephone booth, dispensing movie tickets with a smile that would have scared off King Kong. I tossed her a buck, waved off the change, and stumbled into the cool darkness of a place I hadn't been in years. I used to go to the movies more when I was first getting into the business. They didn't cost a lot, had working latrines, and if you weren't too picky, free meals.

The trick was to look for couples. They'd wander in all lovey-dovey and carrying half a lunch counter. Soon as they sat down food was the last thing on their minds, or in their hands.

Lunch and a floor show, what could be better than that?

Not one of my proudest moments but you gotta take care of things. I think I found every Cracker Jack prize ever made, and developed a large hate for popcorn. You can only eat so much of that crap and not go crazy. I didn't exactly starve but I didn't need bigger pants until I got good enough to buy a desk and hang around Stella's. That was a happy day, what that woman could do to a nickel steak.

That part of my life was long gone thankfully but the memories lingered. I took a pew in the back, lifted a mickey off of some guy passed out next to me, and watched the bullets fly for a couple of hours. Nothing like a good duster to while away the hours, Colman sure knew his way around a six-shooter.

I would have stayed for the third feature but the house lights came on at about six. Some ape of an usher waving a flashlight like it was lit dynamite herded us all out the exit and slammed the door shut. Guess he and the gravel truck wanted to make a night of it and we were in the way.

I had a hankering for something more than caramel corn, so I moseyed on over to Stella's and threw my money down. She didn't so much look at me as grab the cash with one hand and hustle me into a dark corner with the other.

"Hey! I wanna eat, not wrestle. What's with you?" I grumbled.

"Hey yourself you dumbass! You got half the town lookin' for you, again." Her voice seemed a little louder than the usual bullhorn she employed, so you had to know she was a little upset about something. And that something had just wandered into her diner.

"What did you do this time? No, let me guess, not one but two stiffs show up outta nowhere and your name all over both of them! Can't you do anything quietly," she spat.

That got my attention. Here I was thinking the whole world had gone crazy and now this. "I did do it quietly, I mean I didn't do anything, it just happened. So who's lookin'."

"Just about every blue johnny in town. There's even a reward. Couple grand."

"Don't even think about it," I hinted darkly.

"Like I don't have enough trouble. Look, you shouldn't be here. Couple detectives have been around twice already, they could come back at any time. Maybe you want take out?"

"Nah. Not in the mood. I think I'll just stay here and watch the moon come up."

"Fine, fine, but just stay out of sight, will ya? It's almost closing time, but I'll see what I got left."

Serves me right, all I got was meatloaf and mashed potatoes, and no gravy. Here I am licking my chops, ready for something hot and greasy and what do I get, something my gramma used to throw at me. She'd set the plate down, I'd look at her, she'd look at me, and I'd smile and pick up my fork. Nice lady but three times a week was a lot to take. I tried telling her about this thing called a steak once but all it got me was a clip across the back of my head, and a glare that would have melted steel. I sighed, picked up my fork, and smiled grimly.

"So, did you do it?"

"Do what?" I asked between forkfuls.

"Take out Vance. Seems he has a lot of friends, and they're a little pissed at what happened to him."

"So why do they think it was me? I didn't even get my piece out 'til they'd emptied a whole clip at us. I ducked and he didn't. They got him and missed me, that's all I know, I swear."

"Well, that's not how I hear it. Anyways, somebody called in a tip and the word's out, you're top of the wanted list right now, so watch where you walk. And use the back way, I don't want people talkin', I run a respectable joint. Ain't no place for a wanted felon like you."

"Wonderful."

"Not so much. You can't go home either. They went to see your neighbour, the laundry lady, and she threw a tub of hot starch at them. Seems she's on your side, though I can't imagine why."

I sat back and smiled broadly at the thought of Mrs. Chen taking on the Police Department all by herself. She was a real pistol that one, all of five foot nothing and all of it heart. Ran that place of hers with an iron fist and a sharp eye. Laundries were a dime a dozen but hers seemed to have a lock on half the town. Place was always full of heat and steam and brown paper packages coming and going. If I didn't know any better, I'd swear she was making book or running drugs. She wasn't.

As for me, I was in and out of her place so often I was practically family. Most times I was on the run from somewhere or someone, so I could never stay and chat. Just grab an eggroll on the way past, wave a thank you, and then down the fire escape outside her back window. That was usually followed by something loud in Chinese. And there was the soup.

We were just neighbours but she had this thing about me being dressed nice. Not a month would go by without her throwing something at me, socks, pants, a shirt, all of it cleaned and pressed and just my size.

"Listen," said Stella quietly, interrupting my reverie. "I got a couple friends asking after you."

"And they are…"

"No one you need to know. I'm just asking is all, for them. You got any kind of a lead on this? Any idea who it might be? My friends have a need to keep this quiet. This could smooth over if you can figure things out quietly."

"How quietly."

"No headlines, no more bodies, no more questions, just fix it. My friends can be very understanding."

That said a lot. Stella and her friends were not just drinking buddies. They owned things, they were things, and they did a lot of things that no one needed to know about. They weren't saying it but this made my involvement official, my client was now someone who needed my full attention. And, boy, was she was going to get it.

I spent the night huddled in a booth at the back, the only one without a window, the cracked red leather glued to my face. Not exactly the five-star treatment that Stella made her living from but I could see her point. We both needed me alive to get things done, and quickly.

I didn't shoot the cook although I scared the living daylights out of him. All he remembers is peaking around the corner of the end booth, wondering why a pair of feet were there, only to find himself staring at the business end of a worn but still serviceable .45. There was about ten seconds of silence while I woke up enough to recognise who it was. The gun never wavered and neither did he. He aged ten years in that time, or so he kept telling me.

He was Freddie, Stella's cranky old grease monkey.

"Sumbitch, boy, sumbitch! You almos' shoot me! What matter wid you! Did not your mother tell you never point no gun at friend! I point no gun at you, you no point no gun at me! I tell Stella I mad at you!" And so on and so on all the way into the kitchen where the conversation continued loudly with the pots and pans. Tell the truth I don't know all that much about my mom, but Freddie was another story. He and Stella made this little hole in the wall sing, she being the fat soprano and him banging out the chorus with the skillets.

They'd been together for as long as I could remember, long enough to know that he was the real brains of the outfit. Stella had all the charm of a snake, a smile that made people wet themselves, and a right with enough heft to kill a bear. But she couldn't cook past a boiled egg, even the kind that bounce off the floor when you drop them. That's where Freddie came in. He was a tall goomer, thin as a rake, bald, and Chinese. Had some kinda Wing Lang Ling name that not even God could pronounce, so Stella called him Freddie. He specialised in all things greasy and deep-fried, the kind of stuff that made a man's heart sing and his stomach sit up and howl. My kinda cook.

Which is what I got after he calmed down. A nice juicy steak lying under a couple of eggs over easy, and a vat of steaming hot coffee. He didn't know from coffee all that good himself, but he made it strong enough to wake up the dead. Amen to that, brother.

"Ain't you ever gonna learn," groused Stella, coming in just as I was making sur my plate was clean. "Ain't you ever gonna learn not to shoot your friends. You only got like two of them, and if you shoot that one you'll starve to death before you find another." I slapped a deuce into her meaty palm, shot back the rest of the black gold, and made for the door. I wanted to be on the move before the rest of the world started in on me. I wanted to do it to them before they did it to me.

CHAPTER SEVEN

It was a sure bet I couldn't go home. Not only were there a couple of suits lounging around out front, pitching pennies into the back of an old Chevy ragtop, but there was a flatfoot standing on the corner about half a block up. He was dragging on a smoke and trying to look as if he belonged there. He didn't. They rarely patrolled this neck of the woods, especially during the day.

I hit up a corner store for a deck of smokes and a fifth of Scotch. Wasn't about to start the day without them and this was going to be a long one. It was a safe bet Constantine was behind all this, him being the only guy I'd pissed off lately. For a new guy in town he sure had a lot of friends, seemed like every corner had some joker keeping his eyes peeled for yours truly. Not that I couldn't get around town, all those eyeballs just made it a bit more difficult.

I figured my best bet was to find the man himself and put it to him personally. I had a few more questions for that sleazy schmuck, and I kinda liked his taste in booze. Imported, not watered down, and free. Here I am with two murders around my neck and a whole town on the lookout for me, and I show up at his place looking for a refill. The look on his face would be worth the price of admission.

And all because I just couldn't just leave things alone. My client had a name now, something I couldn't have pronounced sober, but the why still wasn't clear. And that bothered me. Like any good dog with a bone, I had a real good chew on my hands and I wasn't about to let go.

That's because you're only human, Sandy would say, giving me that look of hers. The one I didn't like because she knew she was right, and so did I. She'd been down this road with me before and knew what was coming. It's just a part of who you are. Not that you'd ever admit it, but that's okay, it's your one redeeming feature, it's what keeps me hanging around. We all have to believe in something. We all do. Even the worst of us.

I didn't quite see it that way. Say what you want about me, and there were plenty with a lot to say on the subject, I did what I did because it kept me sane, gave me a reason to wake up in the morning. The only difference between me and the dog was what got buried at the end of the day.

I trudged west along the main drag, pulling on a smoke, daring anyone to look me in the eye, when something caught mine. Traffic was stopped cold, everybody with a horn leaning on it to get everybody else moving, time was money. I couldn't see the reason for the delay but what I did see stopped me cold. Those two idiots, the ones that had taken me for a tour of downtown the other day, were right in front of me.

I pitched my smoke, slid my piece out nice and quiet, and made ready to stick it in somebody's ear. Didn't want to spook them, just wanted to get close enough to ask a couple questions. They owed me that much. I'm all for the occasional free ride, but not with a .38 stuck in my ribs, and an invitation to meet the devil's kin. I prefer to make that introduction on my own terms.

I kept my old friend under cover while I worked my way into traffic and started moving upstream to where my friends were waiting. I got close enough to see they were driving an old Dodge Business Coupe, black, with a spare strapped to the back. Not much of a getaway car, guess Petey wasn't as smarmy as he first appeared. Not that it mattered once the mook in the passenger seat decided to see what all the hubbub was about. Half out the window he spotted me tiptoeing up, took all of a second to recognise me, and then it all went to hell.

He started blazing away at me with a peashooter .38, all of it badly aimed. Then traffic started moving and they were on the go, the shooter yelling at the driver to get effing moving, he's seen us. I sprinted after them, trying to get close enough for a clear shot. Maybe if I showed them I was serious they'd think twice about running for it.

Meantime, the effect of six slugs ripping through traffic at random had put the fear of god into everybody else. As my old gran used to say, it was like bedlam let loose on sale day at the Five and Dime. People abandoned their cars and ran every which way, desperate to avoid any more lead coming their way. King Kong was on the loose and out for blood.

I shoved my way through the growing mob but gave it up

after half a block. There was too much bedlam let loose for me to accomplish anything more than bruise my knuckles shoving people out of the way. I could still see them, but they were well ahead and fading fast. Getting up close and personal with Constantine was going to have to wait.

Or was it. I needed wheels to catch up to those two, and there was a set just a block up, idling in front of some apartment block or other. A cab. If anyone knew how to make up time and distance in a hurry, it was a hack. Threw myself in the back and made to pull out my wallet. He looked up at me in the rear view mirror with a face that said I was wasting his time.

"Sorry pal, I'm taken. Waiting for a fare, see. Ya gotta get out."

"What?"

"Yeah, look mac, I gotta sit here and wait for some high 'n mighty to come down with her little doggy. They wanna go shopping or something, so she calls me and pays double just to get a ride for four blocks. Can you believe that?" He shook his head in mock disbelief.

"Look, pal, I'm not going four blocks. I'm after that car over there, the black Dodge two door with the nut hanging out the passenger side. He took a shot at me and I want to return the favour. I'll pay ya double what she's paying, now get moving." I waved what little cash I had under his nose, but nothing doing.

He turned around to face me, more irritated than sympathetic.

"Look, buddy, I'd like to help you out, really I would but...." He found himself staring cross-eyed at the barrel of my gun.

"I said get moving!"

"Okay okay, sheesh!"

The engine roared to life, the tires squealed, and we were off.

"What'd he do, rob a bank?"

"No."

"Jealous husband?"

"No."

"Okay okay, just askin' is all."

"Don't ask, just drive."

We raced through the downtown like Crash Corrigan going to church, the car swaying wildly with each crank of the wheel. Left, right, left, flying over tram rails, screaming around little old ladies out for an afternoon drive. It was all I could do just to stay in my seat.

Ol' Crash hunched over the wheel, squinting through the windshield and puffing away on the fat stub of a stogie. The tip glowed red, matching his determination, but we couldn't get any closer than a block or so.

I tapped him on the shoulder. He looked back briefly.

"Yeah?"

"This is good. If you can keep this distance, just follow them, okay?"

"Whatever you say, pal. Look, you can put that thing away. I'm an ex-cop, I know what a chase is all about, so don't worry about losing him. Worry about what we're gonna do when we get there."

"Yeah?"

"Look, this town ain't that big. He's gonna stop running sooner or later. What do we do when we catch up."

"Leave that to me," I yelled over the blare of angry car horns. "Just keep your foot on the gas."

"No problem."

That being said I sat back and checked on what I actually did have to work with. My .45 and two spare clips. I had a bad habit of lettin' her rip when I pulled the trigger so two clips was cutting it kinda close. He was right, what was I gonna do if we caught up with those two. I couldn't see him getting involved, ex-cop or not, other than to wish me luck as he drove off. Constantine was bound to have a couple of triggers kicking around, so this was going to get real interesting, real quick.

Taking a long pull from my mickey, I passed it up front where Crash did the same and tossed the empty out the window. It was going to be that kind of a chase.

We passed out of the downtown north into a collection of aging warehouses, flophouses, and gin joints. I'd been up here before, and like everything else in this burned-out burg, it was all boarded up windows and broken dreams.

I'd spent most of my last visit to this pleasant end of town standing in the rain, waiting and watching for some sugar daddy and his squeeze to make an appearance. Seems wifey had cottoned onto them and wanted goods enough to divorce his ass and rob him blind at the same time. She didn't care about the squeeze.

Not sure what was in the water but I'd picked up one hell of a cold. Enough to make me sneeze in the middle of a murder. Mine. I roared out a good one and looked up in time to see a radiator coming at me and picking up speed. Sugar Daddy. I think I bounced off the fender but he didn't stop to check and my gunfire got lost in the thunder and lightning. Next day I read about a murder-suicide uptown, wifey's been shot full of holes and sugar daddy's taken one last bath. That's why PIs never get rich.

Our friends cruised around a couple of blocks before pulling up to a brick and timber mountain of a building with boarded up windows and a fire escape missing the escape. They hurried inside while we eased slowly on by, taking a good look. I didn't recognise either of them, not that it mattered much. I had my fingers crossed he was inside, and with a little persuasion, able to talk.

I got my friend to pull over and I stepped out, praying that I knew what I was doing.

"Thanks, pal," I said quietly. "What do I owe you?"

"Forget it. Best time I've had in weeks. Just be careful."

"Yeah, I'll keep it in mind."

He left, and I was alone with a five-story problem and no way in. Shooting my way in was tempting, but even I wasn't that dumb, if only because I didn't know exactly what I was up against. There had to be more goons inside but how many was the question.

I shook out a smoke and wandered around outside, looking for any obvious signs of anything. There weren't any. No names, no numbers, no nothing, just seven stories of dingy grey building, all of it sealed up tight as a coffin. The only promise was the fire escape, but the bottom two stories were lying in a heap in an alley beside the building.

Round and round I went, always coming back to the heap in the alley, like I could bring it back to life somehow. My instincts were screaming at me, the answer is right here, but was I dumb enough to try. Probably. I looked at the two fires escapes through the blue haze of my cigarette smoke, measuring distances and seeing stars. It was nightfall and I was feeling no pain, just crazy.

The answer was right there, in the alley beside the half-wrecked fire escape. The building beside her had the same escape but it was in one piece. And four stories up there couldn't be more than ten feet between the two. I finished my smoke, laughed quietly at myself, hoofed in the front door of the sister building, and followed my gun cautiously into the lobby.

The staircase was wide and inviting, worn smooth with age and the shuffle of countless shoes. Another monument to man's greed and his less than graceful fall when everything caved in on him. On that day, the whole world seemed to stand still, and nobody was safe. Rich and poor jumped out the window together.

Four floors up I turned down a hallway to look for a way across the river Jordan. I didn't think gran would appreciate the thought but the alley seemed just as wide and I had no boat, just a bad idea.

It almost seemed too easy. Find the exit sign, follow it down a dark and dusty hallway to a large casement window that opens onto the fire escape. Crank open said window with a fire axe picked up along the way, and climb out into the cool of an evening breeze. And that's where the plan came up short.

True, the two buildings were pretty much kissing cousins apart, but the river Jordan was four floors down and I couldn't see bottom, even with a match. I practised swearing for a few minutes before climbing back in and considering plan B. Which I didn't have one of.

And what's worse, all this was taking time and that was starting to worry me. I figured if those two goofs were too lazy to worry about being followed then I had advantage enough to make surprise work. But I had to be over there and not over here. It was starting to look like I was going to have to do this the hard way. Again.

The axe and I went looking for inspiration.

What we came up with was a couple of boards from a long narrow table taking it easy in what must have been a clothing business. The whole floor, every corner of it, was heaped with rolls of cloth, sheets of paper, and giant scissors, all covered in a thick layer of dust and draped in cobwebs. The joint had probably jumped with the rich and the famous whining about how this made them look fat or that was the wrong shade. They were long gone, as were the owners, but I swear I could still hear them. Instinct put my hand on my gun, just for a second.

The axe and I worked up a good sweat destroying that part of the past. The result was a pair of ten-foot boards that still had a bit of life in them. We dragged them back down the hall, shoved them out the window, and to my surprise, they reached the other side with inches to spare. Plan B was looking better and better.

So now, all I had to do was climb up onto the railing, and walk across a bridge not much wider than my shoe. You see them do it in the circus all the time. And there's that guy who dances across whole streets on a wire not much bigger than a shoelace. Easy for him, and it might have been for me because I was just as determined, but I made the mistake of looking down and not over.

It was only ten feet or so, but it could have been the Grand Canyon from where I stood. My bridge rattled in the wind, daring me to try its patience and see if I would walk the walk. Wooden bridges aren't always what they seem, last time I crossed one there were huge lakes on either side of it, and it was raining lead. Bombs and bullets fell like hail, throwing up mud and bodies and all the other crap that a battlefield collects.

There was only one way to do this, standing start, run like hell, and leap into the next shell hole before, well, before it's gone too. I wasn't sure I could face that again but that was then and this was now. I'd lost a lot over there, friends, enemies, but mostly my love of life. I didn't have much of a one after that, and I saw no reason to change the situation. I'd had enough.

I took a deep breath, held it in tight, and stepped out into the darkness. The wind seemed louder than before, the other side now lost in the shadows. I wasn't afraid, never was about most things, just had this nagging doubt, a little corner of my brain asking me why. If I knew the answer to that I'd have been rich and retired by now.

Took a second step, looked across and not down, and froze.

Experts say you can conquer your fears by overcoming the worst of them first. This wasn't my worst but it came damn close. It became my worst when I looked across and saw a face in the shadows looking back at me. It peered out of a broken window behind my intended destination, and I could have sworn it waved at me. I sure hoped it was friendly.

Now or never.

Ten feet is no more than three giant steps when you think about it, but I wasn't thinking much beyond the other end of the bridge. Be a helluva way to go, but no one would ever know, or care. They'd just scoop me up and toss me into some hole out back of Potters field, or wherever it was the city buried its lost and found. I took three giant steps, leaping the last one, reaching for the escape even as the bridge bounced one too many times and vanished into the dark below.

"Jesus, that was close," I muttered.

"Damn straight it was, and a damn fool thing to do!" replied a voice. I yanked out my piece, the click of the hammer sparking more conversation.

"No need for that now! No need! I just live here is all, don't have nothin' to shoot for. Just me is all. Don't need no bullets or nothin', just don't shoot."

"Yeah, okay, fine, just come out where I can see you, nice and slow."

"Okay, okay, it's just me, Thomas." A pair of shaky, dirt-streaked hands appeared over the edge of the window, followed by the rest of Thomas. He was a mouse of guy, no bigger than Mrs Chen, scrawny, unshaven, and shaking like a leaf. His clothes said scrounger, wearing whatever he could find, not worrying about the colour or if it made him look too thin. He was already there.

I swallowed hard and put my piece away. I don't know who was more scared, him for just saying hello or me for trying to join the circus. He climbed warily over the sill and joined me out on the fire escape. I thumbed him a smoke and lit it off mine. He looked like he could use one, shaking like it was December, so was I for that matter. He inhaled the stick like it was imported and Cuban, blowing the blue smoke slowly out of his grimy nostrils. Man knew his smokes.

"You weren't really gonna shoot me, were ya?"

"Nah. I'm trying to save money on bullets this month."

Turns out he was the caretaker for the place. Or he was until it had closed down a couple of years back. Had no place else to go so he stayed, sleeping in one of the maintenance rooms on the roof. He made a little money working the streets with hat in his hand, some of the shelters gave him clothes and shoes, but mostly he was on his own.

"It's not too bad," he said, choking down a second smoke. "Not too bad at all. Been awhile since I had one of these. Shelters won't give 'em to ya, run by all them holy rollers and such. They don't like smokers and drinkers so I don't go there unless I hafta. Most of these places are empty now so I can get pretty much anything else I need."

"Like what, pencils? " I asked, half joking. "Can't eat those."

"Nope, but you can sell 'em. Lot of people still need pencils these days. Paper too. Tried chairs once but a cop saw me and chased me off. Called me a thief. I ain't a thief, I just use what other people don't want no more. Man's gotta eat, right?"

"Yeah, I hear ya buddy. Keep the smokes." I flipped him the rest of the deck.

"Geez, thanks pal! Hey, these are the good ones! Can't afford them. Gotta buy rebuilds offa ol' Billy, only his eyesight ain't too good no more. Don't always know what's in 'em. Got any matches?" I handed those over.

"So, what can you tell me about this place? Anybody inside?"

"You ain't the law, is ya?"

"Nope. PI, working a case. So, who's inside, Tommy."

"Thomas."

"Sorry, Thomas. So, who's inside? Followed a coupla guys over this way and watched them go in the front door. Ain't seen 'em come out yet. You know where they're at?"

"Yep."

"Care to enlighten me?"

He took a long drag, savouring the taste of the blue smoke, before gently easing it out of his nostrils. With his eyes closed and a smile out to here, I had a friend for life. Me, I practically lived on the things but they never had that effect on me.

"Third floor at the back, right beside the east stairwell. Took over old man Lowenstein's office, gotta real sweet setup, desks, chairs and all. Even got a working phone … oh ... and a safe."

"No kiddin'?"

"Nope. Watched them bring up it on the elevator. Big sucker. Gotta be a ton at least, all black, big dial on the front. Don't know what they keep in it, but it's gotta be pretty important, don't 'cha think?"

"Yeah I think. How's about you showing me where it's at. Wouldn't mind getting a closer look."

"Sure thing pal, anything you want."

"And keep the noise down, okay, I want this to be a surprise."

"Gotcha."

Pulling out my friend with the faded bluing, I followed Thomas inside. We crept along a dusty hallway, went around some corners, down more stairs, and came to a halt outside a wood panelled door with glass top half. Like mine. Right on the glass in dusty black lettering, Lowenstein and Sons Barristers and Solicitors. I never could figure out what the hell kind of lawyer that actually was, I just knew them as pains in the ass, all of them.

And beyond the door, voices.

Now came the eternal question PIs always ask themselves, do I go in shooting or hang back in the shadows and wait. Personally, there's nothing I like more than to pound down a door and shoot whatever's behind it, but I've got company today. He's good people is Thomas, wouldn't hurt a fly, but I do this kind of stuff alone. I'm as likely to shoot him as anybody else once things heat up, so the door got a reprieve.

Meantime, Thomas had started cleaning a corner of the window with his sleeve, looking to eyeball what was on the other side. I grabbed a fistful of collar and dragged him quickly and quietly back up the stairs we'd just come down.

He gave me the international what gives sign with his hands. I pointed to the floor with my gun and made the international we're not going back down there until they leave first sign with my left hand. He gave me a thumbs-up and sat back against a wall. Pulled out a flask and took a jolt of something that made his eyes pop, then passed it on to me.

I took a long pull of his joy juice and spent the next minute or so trying not to cough up a lung. She was smooth as silk going down, a definite lip smacker, followed by a minor forest fire in the belly, definitely not your grandmother's afternoon tea. He nodded at me with this what did I tell you it's the best ever look on his face, and gave me two thumbs up when I could finally see straight. I had to hand it to Tommy boy, I'd just taken a shot of the best Potato champagne on the planet.

It's the kind of stuff shiners cooked up in every henhouse, doghouse, and outhouse in the country. All you needed was a pot, a fire, potatoes and some patience, and you could fly a rocket to the moon with the stuff. And it did wonders for whatever else might ail you, an ounce or two of this and you wouldn't feel anything for a very long time.

He crawled over, this big goofy grin on his face, and crouched at my feet like a good little doggie waiting for a treat or something. We spoke in whispers. I smiled through my tears, handing his juice back as carefully as a live grenade minus the pin. Glad you liked it, he whispered, got a whole crock of it up on the roof, it's not my best but I got more cooking. No wonder he looked like a dead horse come to life when he tipped it back.

Patience is not my strong suit. This sitting on my ass waiting for something to happen, drives me crazy, always has. It's a wonder I'm still alive considering how many times I've said to hell with it and just did what needed doing. Maybe I'd mellowed a little, if you could call it that. Could be I was a bit more patient than I used to be, or maybe I'd learned that doing something rash wasn't always my best play. Half a pack of smokes later I was all for putting my size nines to use, and shooting whatever moved.

Thomas was long gone up to the roof, gotta check on my next batch he said quietly, still smiling hard. Good luck with that I thought, as I waved him off, and for god's sake finish that smoke first, you don't want to be the first man on Mars. He must have read my mind because he was back after butt number ten hit the floor and I was rechecking the slide on my piece.

"They's done," he said, smiling crookedly. "They drove off 'bout a minute ago. Saw 'em from the roof. It's safe to go down now."

"That's good to know. Thanks. So tell me," I asked, looking at him a little sideways. "How the hell does a guy like you get all the way down here in less than a minute. It's gotta be like six floors, right?"

"Oh, yeah, yeah, it's seven. I used the elevator."

"What elevator. I didn't hear nothing."

"Can't, it's made of water."

I looked at him like he'd just told me the Empire State building was made of cheese.

"Yeah, it's got water in it. You pull on one rope and it fills a tank and you go up. You pull the other rope and it fills another tank and you go down. Easy as pie. That's how they got the safe in here."

"Really, you just pull on the rope and up she goes."

"Yep. The water doesn't make any noise, see. There's another one around the corner, same thing, no noise. They used to have horses in here, and horses get spooked by motors so water does the trick and up they go. It's kinda like a toilet flushing, only without all the other stuff."

"Zat a fact?" I asked, not sure if he was pulling my leg or not.

"Yep. Used to be a delivery business on the main floor, used horses 'til they got a truck."

"Fair enough. Now, I don't know about you, but I'm a little too curious for my own good. I'm gonna go and see what's in that safe. So, here's the thing I like you Thomas, you're a good guy, don't want you getting hurt on my account so I want you to stay here and hold the fort."

"Gotcha, chief!"

The door, propelled by size nine shoe leather, slammed open, exploding the glass panel and burying the door knob in the wall to my right. I stepped into the office cocked and locked and ready for anything, the barrel of my old friend sweeping the room like a hound dog casting for a scent.

Immediately in front of me was a massive oak desk, the top shiny as a new penny.
Off to the left a couple of straight-back wooden chairs, the good kind with leather seats, a floor lamp, coatrack, and up against the far wall Thomas' ton of steel, its doors wide open. A small throw rug on the floor, paintings on the wall, and you had a Norman Rockwell moment.

Standing in the middle of this welcoming scene, on the far side of the desk facing the safe, stood a snazzy grey suit. It didn't move a muscle but I recognised the smarmy attitude. Constantine.

"Well, hello," I said, smiling stiffly. "Didn't think a guy like you slummed it up like this. You get lost on your way to the club or something?"

"Ahhh, Mister Ford," he purred, not brave enough to turn around.

"Same as last time. Now don't do anything you might regret. I don't like you all that much so it wouldn't take much to do something I wouldn't."

"You are very persistent, Mister Ford. Troublingly so. Especially where things don't concern you. Might I ask the reason for your visit this time?"

"You might. And I might just tell you. Now turn around and sit down."

"Might I be allowed to close the door to my safe? This is not the best of neighbourhoods. Too many, um, how shall I say… undesirables about?"

"Yeah, well, I desire you to leave the door open. I'll make sure nothing happens to it."

"You are too kind." And with that he turned around slowly and sat in what must have been old Lowenstein's chair. It creaked as he sank back into its padded leather comfort. He steepled his fingers in front of him, elbows resting on the padded arms of the chair. There was this thoughtful look on his face, like the one I get from judges on occasion. They never know what to do with me either.

Usually I got off with a warning or a small fine, but he didn't strike me as the understanding type. He would probably sentence me to a running start.

Me, I straddled one of the office chairs backwards, arms folded across the top, staring right back at him, gun in hand, daring him to so much as twitch. Judges didn't like that attitude either, but there was no bailiff around to kick me upright. Not that I didn't trust the guy, I didn't.

After a few moments of silence, he took a deep breath and sat back further in the chair. It groaned ominously with the effort.

"Well now, aren't we at a pretty pass, my friend. I'm unarmed, as you can see, so should I be calling for help? Unfortunately, that means you would probably shoot me. In which case, you would be unable to call for help, as my men would most certainly shoot you. So here we are. Tell me Mister Ford, just what is the price of your persistence."

I lit up while I thought about that. Blew a couple of smoke rings his way.

"I'm not greedy. Just a little information is all. You give me that, and we can all be on our merry little way."

"Ah. And that comes with a price also, as I am sure you are aware. I am a man of humble means, but surely we can come to some sort of agreement? I have certain resources I could send your way."

"Yeah, I appreciate the offer but that's not why I'm here."

"Really? I'm most impressed, an investigator with a conscience. You are a rarity."

"Tell that to my bookie. He'd appreciate the sentiment."

He smiled wickedly. "Now, what information would I have that might possibly interest you."

"It's about the girls…"

He stared at me darkly, as if I'd just said the magic words to open Ali Baba's cave. "What girls."

CHAPTER EIGHT

"What do you mean, what girls," I growled. "The dead ones, you know, the ones you leave in an alley like a dead dog. What was her name … oh yeah … Adelaida. I call her Addy for short. A knife in the ribs and a dark alley to die in. Helluva thing. You bring 'em all the way from wherever and the second it goes wrong they end up dead. I can understand that it's just business and all but I gotta problem with that. See, thing is they're blaming me for that little problem and I didn't do it. You know that and I know that, and oh yeah, there's that little matter of the lawyer you hired to handle the paperwork. He's dead and I didn't do that either, and you know that, too, don't you."

A thin smile crept across his lips.

"But more important is the why. Why go to all that trouble and then off her when things go a little off the rails? What'd she do to you, or maybe it was something she didn't do, is that it? I'm just dying to know, just like she was, only I'm harder to kill."

He put his hands flat on the desk in front of him, leaned forward and slowly got up. His eyes never left mine, like he was daring me to do something stupid, or deadly, or both. I let him have his moment, I'd waited long enough for this so I could wait a little longer. I needed answers, not another body in the morgue.

"You flatter yourself, Mister Ford. You come all this way and only have it half right, and you expect me to do your work for you and tell you all. Really, I'm surprised at you, a man with your reputation. I would have thought the rest was obvious, clearly your talents aren't what they should be, or I'd be under arrest by now."

I flicked my butt away and rose to the challenge, taking him on eyeball to eyeball.

"Your singular pursuit of this case, as you call it, intrigues me," he said with a smirk. "There are thousands of women in this city, so why her. What is it about her that captures your attention so, you owe me at least that much before you kill me. And you are going to kill me, are you not?"

"I don't owe you anything."

"Nor I you."

Constantine had this look on his face, one that I'd seen before, in another time and place, one that set off alarm bells that I was too slow to answer. He turned to his left towards the open safe, making this grand gesture like he was about to raise the dead or vanish in a puff of smoke.

"I have nothing to hide my friend, take what you will, you may yet find what you are looking for."

Shmuck that I am I just stared at him, watching him and not his eyes. Ever read about cowboys and how they claim they can read a man's eyes, know when he's gonna draw? Well, it's pretty much all true. They flicker just before something happens, which gives you about a split second head start. Trick is you have to be watching the eyes to catch it.

I was too busy watching Petey and missed the flicker. He was right in front of me and I didn't see it. One second he's waving his magic wand around and the next his left hand disappears inside his coat pocket. It comes out like a snake with one bite left clutching a snub nosed .38, aimed in my general direction. A neat trick, but who would have thought he was a lefty. Didn't come across too many of those in my line of work, most of the shooters I knew were righties, and dead.

He slowly turned to face me again, arm steady like any decent shooter should.

"So, here we are Mister Ford. I appear to have the drop on you, as they say. Speaking of which, you may drop that… thing any time," he growled, gesturing at the contents of my right hand with his peashooter. I stood up slowly, eyes locked on his, the chair to my left.

"Guns make me nervous, really they do. They can be so dangerous in the wrong hands."

"I can see that, and the answer's no. You want it, you'll have to come over here and take it off me." It wasn't in me to give up, let alone gracefully, I've stared down deadlier moments and walked away.

"I would much rather you bring it here," he growled.

"My arms don't reach that far."

"Well then, that can only mean one thing …"

There was a loud bang as the door in the next office slammed open. Thomas. Right time, wrong door. Constantine jerked slightly at the noise, there was a sharp crack and a shot went over my right shoulder. My left hand heaved the chair up at him even as my right came up and tried to take aim. The chair bounced off the desktop and slammed into him, throwing his aim off just slightly.

I fired and missed, moving fast to the right, keeping the desk between us. He followed the movement, firing as fast as he could, filling the room with gun smoke and lead. At the end, we fired together, two roars of anger aiming to finish this quickly and painfully. I hit him in the chest, throwing him back against the open safe, a surprised look on his face. I spun around as he creased my left shoulder, the impact throwing me to the floor.

Surprise turned to a snarl as his peashooter took aim at me again, wavering slightly as his life drained out of him. It was all I could do to empty my clip in his general direction, and hope to hit more than thin air. Shots came in rapid succession until the hammer clicked on empty, more gun smoke and lead crowding into the office. Old Lowenstein would not have been impressed with the cavalier treatment of his office digs.

Turns out I had more than hope on my side. Nine rounds, five holes. I counted. Falling to his knees, Constantine then tipped forward onto the floor. His expression didn't change on the way down, as if dying was the least of his worries. Maybe not for him, but it sure was for me. My only other witness was now my third murder charge. I was going to do life and then some.

"Wow, he dead?" asked Thomas, staring wide-eyed at the wreckage, peering around the edge of the door like a ghostly Kilroy.

"Yeah, that happens sometimes. Sorry about the noise."

"Heck no, don't worry about me. I'm used to that. I hear all kinds of noises."

"I'll just bet you do."

"Yeah, I do. Say listen, uh, it's getting kinda late and I kinda gotta be somewhere, you know. If I don't somebody else will get the day olds, and I'll get the crusts. I kinda don't like that. Not much to 'em and I'm kinda hoping they got sourdough. Today's Tuesday and they do sourdough on Tuesdays. Is it Tuesday today?"

"Might be, not too sure myself. Listen, you go now and don't worry about me, I'll lock up. And hey…Thomas."

"Yeah?"

"Thanks. Things can get a little messy, doing what I do, but it's real important what we did today, you and me. Thanks, pal."

"Hey, any time." He threw this great big goofy grin at me.

"And don't worry about this," I said, kicking the late Mister Constantine. "I'll find him a good home."

"Okey dokey, see ya later."

My shoulder stung like hell but it was only a nick, one of more than a few that I'd ever admit to. Mrs Chen wouldn't be too thrilled to have more of her hard work shot to pieces, but we'd been down this road before. I could count on a scolding and a new shirt, both delivered in Chinese. I slammed in my last clip and holstered my piece.

Heaved the corpse of the day onto his back and gave him the once over, ignoring the stunned look on his face. I don't suppose he'd figured death would come to him this quickly, most people don't. Lady Luck can take only so much of a joke before she gets a little cranky. She's got one helluva temper, I'd seen it enough times to know. I was hoping the next joke wasn't on me I wasn't done with this life just yet.

Luckily I'd missed all the important stuff, like his cigarette case. It was a nice silver job with his initials on the front, including a full load of Dunhill's, a rich man's stick. They were smooth as a joy girl's caress when she's reaching for your wallet. Me, I want to feel the fire when I suck one back, but who was I to argue, free smokes always went down better. I smiled, lit one up, and savoured the moment.

It was kind of him to have some cash on him, not to mention a very expensive pocket watch and fob, pen, and car keys. Couldn't tell what make but that didn't matter, it had to be close by and I could use a ride home. Like Thomas said it was getting late, and this wasn't the nicest part of town.

Sat down on a corner of the desk, took a couple of deep drags and exhaled heavily, adding to the blue smoke already drifting lazily around the room. Could have used some of his classy hooch, these things always got the heart pounding. Sadly the place was drier than a church on a Monday. Two full smokes later and my composure had returned.

I stepped over the object of no one's desire and stood in front of the open doors of his safe. She was a big one, six-foot doors, four sliding bolts the size of my arm, and a tumbler that took both hands to spin. Not that it mattered, closed or open I knew a guy who could open these things in his sleep. Fritz Knoffler.

He was a German from the old country who'd gone through the same hell as me, only on the other side. Come peacetime he wasn't keen on staying and starving, so he came over here and ended up in this happy little dustbowl. When he couldn't get a job building safes he did the next best thing.

He was a cracksman, and a damn good one. There wasn't a safe, lock, deadbolt, or fastener that he couldn't open. Home was a bookstore in some out of the way corner, hardback and paperback, all of it in German, Austrian, and god knows what else. He was lucky if he sold a book a week but no one questioned how he managed to stay in business. Or why he had such a well-equipped tool room out back of his shop.

Every once in a while, I'd get a case that required his special talents. He'd give me the slightest of smiles when I told him what kind of safe it was. Alongside the card index for the little library he maintained, was another index of all the known safe and lock types in town. He'd show me a card or two, when I covered one with a twenty, he'd simply ask when and where.

I swear the man had ten magic fingers. He went out with me on a job couple months back, and it was all over in fifteen minutes. Husbands can be such idiots, especially when there's a cute little something on the side. This dame hired me to get the goods on hubby but all I had to do was whistle up Fritz.

He pulled out a diamond necklace, probably meant for Cutie Pie, and I gave it to the missus as proof of her suspicions. She swore a little when she saw it, then smiled wickedly, and made sure to wear it the very next night. Soon as hubby saw the glitter, he pulled out his chequebook and paid her off. Easiest two C-notes I ever made.

So, what was Constantine really up to, what was it that had cost Addy her life? I was hoping there was something in this steel closet that would explain it all, to me and to the police. I wasn't on the wall in the Post Office just yet, and I wanted to keep it that way. I didn't have any friends downtown anymore, that bridge had burned a long time ago.

The safe offered up plenty of room but not much else. Clean as a whistle and all but empty, Constantine had been busy packing. Most of the contents were jammed into a large brown leather satchel parked beside the desk. Loose papers spilled out of the top of it, spattered with blood. Seemed right somehow.

Time was running short. His two bully boys were gone but you had to figure they'd be back soon. No self-respecting mastermind ever travelled alone, especially one with an ego like his. And they weren't going to be thrilled when they figured out it was me killed their paycheque.

I didn't know whether to laugh or cry. I'd really counted on getting some answers out of him. And there weren't going to be any, at least from him. All I had was his case, and the faint hope that it contained anything more than his laundry bill.

One thing before I left, a trick I'd picked up from a colleague long since dead. He called it the art of distraction, I called it poetic justice. Half the town was looking for me, so I didn't think Constantine would mind helping to muddy the waters a little, take some of the heat off. All I needed was a window.

Dumping his elegant corpse out a hallway window pretty much gassed me, he was that much of a dead weight. He left a trail of bloody streaks across the floor a blind man could have followed, but once he was out the window the blind man wouldn't have cared. And that included the next flatfoot to wander by.

They all knew what it meant, finding some poor shmuck in an out of the way place, with more holes in him than Swiss cheese. A suspicious circumstance but with a hundred clams found in his breast pocket, there would be no questions asked, just a quick trip to the morgue. Identification might take months, if at all, followed by a hole in the ground somewhere at the City's expense. The lucky lottery winner would buy his missus more flowers and candy than she could ever hope for or imagine. That's why I paid taxes.

It was well after dark when I slipped out the front door, and moved cautiously down the street. I had Peter's bulging satchel in one hand and the keys to his wheels in the other. I was hoping the keys knew the way home because I didn't, and I wasn't about to ask the neighbourhood flattie. He'd have a lot of questions and I wasn't in an answering mood.

The wheels were easy enough to spot, there weren't that many Auburn V-twelves floating around town. Parked under a streetlamp less than a block away, that gorgeous electric blue number just had to be his. My lucky day. A Boat-Tail Speedster had to be just the sweetest ride going, longer legs than a showgirl, and more go power than a dog at the track. And I had the keys. I got weak at the knees just thinking about it. Last time I'd seen iron this heart-stopping, the driver had tried to run me over with it.

The twelve cylinders hiding under the hood fired up without a hitch and settled into a quiet rumble. I flicked on the spotlights and shot off into the night. We flew through the dimly lit streets like an eagle off a mountain, swift and silent and deadly. I could have driven her all night but I gave myself about an hour, we had to be at the Four Aces before it closed.

The Four Aces auto garage was a mid-sized gear-heads paradise, tucked away in an alley just north of the PNR station. A grease monkey named Stinger Martin ran the place. Took in anything with wheels and a motor, and performed a kind of magic with a wrench that had them lining up around the block. It was also the place to go if you had a set of wheels hotter than a volcano's lips.

He had his head inside the hood of an older model Hudson Town car when I rolled in. He whistled in deep appreciation as we slipped smoothly into an empty service bay. I almost cried when I killed the ignition and flipped him the keys.

Stinger ran a practised eye over the double-waxed finish, as much in awe of the moment as I had been when I first saw her.

"Well, lookee here, where did you get this little number. Ain't seen one of these in a while."

"Don't ask."

"Kinda figured that. Come on into the office, I gotta couple beers on ice."

"Sounds good to me." Grabbed the luggage and followed him in.

Stinger pulled a couple of cold ones out of a cooler behind his desk and tossed me one. He threw himself into the only chair in the office and popped the cap off on the edge of the desk.

"Nice place you got here," I said, looking for a place to sit.

"Yeah, I kinda like it. Make yourself to home, I ain't too fussy."

I carved a hole in a mountain of magazines, calendars, and cases of motor oil heaped up in a corner.

"So, what's new?" he asked, taking a long pull. "Haven't seen you for a couple of weeks, not since that last job when you shot up that Packard. Thanks by the way. I spent about a week on her and charged the dumb schmuck for two. And he paid in cash. But did you have to shoot the carburettor, took me forever to get it right."

"Sorry, next time I'll aim for the driver."

"You do that."

We went way back, Stinger and I. Chewed the same dirt you might say, though not over there. He had more oil than blood in his veins, had this knack for making an engine do the impossible. Raced cars and motorcycles until the track turned to horses, dumped his winnings into an old beat up garage, hooked up with Margie and the rest was history.

"So, how's Margie and the kids these days. Nicki's, what, eight now, nine?"

"Nine, and full of pep and ginger just like her mother. Helluva kid," he sighed. "Thing is Margie's kinda not talking to me right now. Seems I associate too much with guys like you or some damn thing, and that scares her a little. Anyways, she's gone to her mother's for a couple days so I'm batchin' it."

"So, what is it this time, she doesn't like the way I look or something?"

"Nah. It's more what you do that pisses her off, like that thing out there. I know I can get five hundred for her easy, but Margie's afraid the cops'll take me in and leave her in a jam. I keep telling her we got loads of cash, I even tell her where I stash the stuff but she won't touch it, some kinda moral code. Anyways, enough on that, what do you want me to do with her." He waved his beer in the direction of my new wheels.

"Do that voodoo that you do so well, my friend, and make her disappear."

"Done. It'll be gone by daylight. How much you want for it. I got about a hundred on me, but I can get more tomorrow."

"Keep it, for Margie and the kids. Call it a finder's fee, just so long as nobody finds it."

"You sure? That's nice, Tone, real nice, but I can handle it, you know that."

"Yeah, I know, just do me a favour is all." I sighed heavily. I'd been getting the evil eye from Margie of late, a sure sign I wasn't welcome anymore. I'd been down this road before, with him and with her, but he and I had been unwilling to let it go, until now. At least I was.

"Anything. Name it."

I took a deep breath and let it all out, hard. "Look, go see her tonight, make it up to her. Do whatever she wants. Tell you're sorry, tell her you'll shoot me on sight, just don't trade her in for me, I ain't worth it."

He stared hard at his beer for a moment. "Yeah, funny thing, we've been talking about that, me and her, but we're pals, go way back, I can't just walk away. Can I?" He looked at me from behind his beer, he'd already decided to fire me, but I'd just beaten him to the punch. That's how it is sometimes with pals.

"Look, I appreciate all you do for me but it's gotta end sometime, you know that, I know that. You got too much good in you to waste it on an ingrate like me. You got family, you got kids, I get that, and so does she. I know I said this last time, but now I mean it I got someone else on tap so don't worry about me, I'll be okay."

My fault more than anything, I was so wrapped up in the pleasure of the drive I'd clean forgotten I'd banned myself from Stinger's. Old habits die hard so I'd showed up one more time, although Margie wouldn't see it that way. And that was the last thing I wanted right now, her to see me here and go after me again. I had enough people on my tail without adding the fury of a wife denied to the mix. It would be safer back in the trenches.

Stinger took a long pull on his beer and stood the empty on the desk next to the others he'd already finished. There was a lot of thinking lined up in front of him. "Yeah, you might be right, you know. I been kinda thinking hard on this, last couple days. I'm doing good without the other stuff, you know. Maybe I don't need that no more, and she does make a helluva apple pie."

"And you got something better going?"

He didn't and he knew it. I liked him, liked what he had, even if he was too dumb to know that sometimes. Margie was good people, he was lucky to have her and the kids. We got along okay, her and I, but you couldn't blame her for not wanting a guy like me hanging around, giving her man bad ideas. Best I take my business elsewhere, the doghouse was starting to get a little crowded.

"Say listen, you still got that rack out back, right?" I asked. "Mind if I crash on it for a couple hours? I can't exactly go home right now."

"Sure, no problem. Just throw my stuff on the floor. I'll get it in the morning. Meantime, I think I'll go for a little walk and see what's what. Maybe she's cooled off by now, this batching ain't much fun, no offense."

"None taken."

Crashed for a couple of hours on Stinger's old army cot and dreamed the dream of going home alive. It was always the same I was home and I was alive but that was where it ended. Seemed I'd traded in one form of combat for another, one where you couldn't always see your enemy or call in any kind of support. You went out alone and if you were real lucky you got back alive. And still alone. Only to do it all over again the next day. Was that skill, luck, or just the stubbornness of being a survivor?

Don't know what time it was when dreamland kicked me out but I snapped right out of it and sat up, gun in hand. Felt like I'd slept for a week, a luxury I'd been missing lately. Threw some water over my face, borrowed Stinger's razor and did what I could to pretty myself up. I hadn't been home for a couple of days and it was starting to show. Been a while since I'd stepped into army green but that's all Stinger had to change into after Margie hoofed him.

The upside to all this was waiting for me right outside Stinger's front door. There's this guy got a stand-and-eat that sells the best dogs on the face of the earth. Great big things the size of a telephone pole, hot off the grill and heaped with all the fixins. He gave Stella a run for her money even though she didn't have them on the menu. I do quality stuff, she'd say, you don't want to know what's in that crap. Hot and greasy covered it as far as I was concerned.

Chewed my way through three of the things and downed a couple shots of mother's milk that came with my coffee. Best thing in the world to wake you up and get you on your feet. Most of these guys had a gallon or two on board and were more than happy to top up your joe.

These stands were everywhere downtown, drove the city fathers nuts. As often as they were swept off the streets they would come back harder and faster. And it wasn't just dogs on board, there was fruit, vegetables, pies, beer, fresh bread, you name it. A guy could walk from one end of the main drag to the other without setting foot in a diner and eat like a king. And they all had something else on the go, numbers, booze, horses, whatever you wanted, no questions asked.

Slapping a five into an open palm got me a ride to nowhere while I figured out my next move. I had a puzzle to solve, some of the pieces, and kind of an idea what it looked like, but that was it. What I really wanted, what I really needed, was someone or something to get me off the hook for the two murders I was probably already pegged for. Constantine was dead but there was no way of pinning that on me, at least directly. My name was bound to come up if there was any investigation, but that was nothing new.

Truth is, I had a case full of possibilities sitting on my lap and no one downtown I could trust with it. I show up with all this and I get a room at the crowbar hotel. Who'd believe a sad sack PI with a bad rep and a half-cocked story about a dead woman and what she might have been up to. Nothing, they would say, you got nothing. And then I'd be cuffed and stuffed and thrown into some deep, dark hole somewhere to contemplate the error of my ways. The end of another mouthy PI who said too much and knew too little.

I sat back and tried to jam the pieces together but they weren't enough of a fit to make any sense. There was more to this puzzle, there had to be, I really hoped the mess on my lap had them. I lit up a Lucky out of the pack I'd taken from Stingers stash, enjoying the quiet while my hack drove wherever the road took him. We watched the town wake up and pretty itself for another day at the grind. After two full smokes of quiet contemplation I tossed an address over the front seat and took my troubles to your friendly neighbourhood money man.

There were a lot of those in town but I wanted Joey Fishbein, an uptown accountant and a damn good one. The man had a singular talent for names and numbers, most of which he forgot as soon as the job was done. He worked hard and got paid well but that was it. It didn't pay to have a long memory in his line of work.

He had an office on the main floor of a three-storey walk-up further out towards the ritzy side of town, no name and no number. Either you knew where he was or it didn't matter. He lived in the front half, worked in the back half, with a solid wall between the two. Didn't like to mix business with pleasure, so he'd walled up the door between, leaving him to focus on the one or the other.

Whatever it was, his office was as sweet a setup as any I'd ever seen. Made me wish I'd worn my good suit and not slept in this one. The place was out of a catalogue, teak furnishings, plush carpeting, velvet seats, the works. The man worked alone, had a girl, a distant cousin I think, come in twice a week to type his correspondence, but that was it. Place was as spotless as his reputation. And no booze, I swear the man lived on bread and water.

As usual he was nose deep in paperwork, didn't see or hear me until the floor creaked an alarm. That look of surprise turned into a welcoming smile, hands clasped in front of him like Joe Louis had just won another round. Probably the only guy in town who really was glad to see me. I held up my problem and gave him a you got time for this look. He nodded enthusiastically.

"Anthony, old friend, long time no see. What brings you around? Oh, wait, I see it, a mystery bag! Oh joy, and I thought this was going to be another day full of tedium and torts." He was on his feet and around the desk to greet me before the door closed behind me. Glad-handed me like I was his long-lost uncle with a fat inheritance to share, traded me a very good stogie for the bag, and left me to sink back in a sofa covered with real leather.

Didn't say a thing, just dumped it out, ignored the blood spatters, and got to work. All business this one, even when I showed up unannounced. Told me once that whenever I showed up I made his day I just reeked of danger and he couldn't wait for me to throw some of it his way. Accounting isn't exactly a glamour job, Anthony. And mine was?

At first glance he didn't come across as a numbers man. He had what they call that movie star quality tall, handsome, rugged good looks, black wavy hair, all the stuff women fainted over. Married to his work and the theatre, of which he was a generous patron. When he wasn't balancing somebody's books, or figuring out where the money was buried, he was out and about at this theatre or that. He couldn't act worth a damn but it was the atmosphere, he said, nothing like it.

Watching Joey work his magic was better than theatre. Each item gently tugged free of the pile, rubbed gently between manicured fingertips, eyeballed, and placed carefully on his desk like it was nitro. Slow and deliberate, everything in its place and a place for everything. Except for the bottle at the bottom of the case. Figures that Constantine wouldn't travel without something smooth and expensive. It sailed my way, underhand, did I mention he played softball on weekends?

That done, Joey crossed his arms, leaned over his desk and looked it over like he was planning to invade something. He nodded thoughtfully every so often, gave this and that a closer inspection, then eventually sat down and went over things in more detail. All this took time, which I didn't have a whole lot of. I made the best of it, sipping more of Constantine's money, and trying to bounce very expensive smoke rings off the gleaming white ceiling.

It was some little time before he looked up, smiled at me, then sat back in his chair.

"So?" I growled.

"So, quite something what you have here, I must say." He

was smiling like a cat with the fattest rat in the barn under his paw.

"Really?" I asked, sitting up straight. I'd seen him wear this look before, something big was in the works and he'd found it. It was the moment he lived for, and the one I was hoping for, the big reveal that was going to get me out from under the heap of trouble I was in. As long as the rat under his paw was Constantine.

"Really, my friend, a hell of a thing. I won't ask where this all came from but I can guess. My advice, run, don't walk, to the nearest exit. Get on the next bus out of town and don't look back."

"That bad?"

"In a word, yes."

Joey had a thing for the dramatic, always waving his arms like he was trying to stop a runaway train, or herd cats somewhere. Today it was an orchestra, his pen waving all over the paper like it was about to start singing. I was sure hoping it was a tune I could work with.

"Mind cluing me in on what's so bad, I'm kinda on the clock on this one. You might even say lives are at stake." Well, mine was anyways.

"Well, that wouldn't surprise me, seeing what I have here. Get them to pay you first. And then go, quickly."

"Like you're always telling me, I'll take that under advisement. Meantime, what have you got?" I got up off the sofa and put one of his velvet seats to work, joining him in his invasion planning.

"A sweet little racket, my friend. Makes lots of money and hurts a lot of people, especially the nosy ones. I've seen this before, but not on this scale. I can't say where I saw it, just that I have. And that's between you and me."

CHAPTER NINE

So, Constantine was no lightweight, I'd figured that, but who else was involved I wondered. This kind of thing took time and money and I wondered where he'd gotten his. Somebody local had their fingers in this pie and they weren't going to be happy with me sniffing around. They were bound to come after me with a fork, or worse.

"Noted. So, what are we looking at?"

Joey took a deep breath and let it out slowly before giving the lowdown.

"This, Anthony, is essentially a tidy little enterprise that robs people of their money, and their dignity. It takes time and money and connections to work properly, and this particular one seems to have all of those. What all this paper tells me is that it extends all the way back to the old country. It details a method for getting people out of the old country and into this country, getting well paid at both ends for doing so."

"It appears to focus on women, for the most part, those that have some money, maybe some family somewhere. They pay through the nose to get here, those without further funds get traded or sold to whomever wants them, and get put to work doing whatever their buyer wants. Prostitution sadly, although some end up as maids or servants, but it's all the same in the end. They have no money and no papers and because of that they can be gone in a moment. Helluva thing, my friend, truly sad."

"Yeah, I got that impression, but how do I deal with it? I'm already up to my neck in it and nothing to go on. You sure those books don't have anything I can use? A name, address? It's kinda important."

"Yes and no. This," he said sweeping his open palms over it like a Sunday blessing, "tells me what and how, but not who or why. That's in these journals here." He tapped a beautifully manicured index finger on a pair of brown leather books off to his right. "These, no doubt, are a record of who and how much, but as I expected, they are coded."

A good accountant, the crooked kind, will do that faithfully keep his masters records in apple pie order but code the entries so if they fall into the wrong hands, nada. The secret was a codebook, something he wore next to his skin, the one item he would take to his grave before giving up. It translated all the chicken scratches into English, something known only to him, and which he would share with the boss only when they were alone. He went on.

"My friend, something like this can cause a lot of trouble if it is ever revealed. Whoever this is," he said, tapping the books again, "has more than a few friends in the right places. They could make a lot of trouble for you."

"That's never bothered me before. I don't exactly have a lot of friends in this town, present company excepted."

He smiled wickedly. "I know enough about you to have you killed, just like that!" he said snapping his fingers at me.

"Thanks. Nice to know I have such considerate friends. You will give me a head's up when you figure it out, right?"

"As always. I can always count on you to break up the tedium of my day with something choice, and this certainly is it. I shall devote my entire waking life to the discovery of its secrets," he chirped. Joey was a like a kid in a candy store with the owner gone home for the day. He wasn't leaving until he had it all in his hands. "So, what are you going to do, my friend?"

"I'm not entirely sure. Thing is I've got a couple murders to think about, and I was kinda hoping this stuff might get me off the hook. I'll take anything you can get me, they don't exactly like me downtown."

"And they will deny the whole thing, claim you made it up, falsified records and so on, and you will disappear my friend, forever."

"Yeah, I kinda figured that too, but that's what I get paid for." Not what I was hoping to hear.

Joey leaned forward in chair, a seriousness to his face. His palms were flat on the paperwork.

"Unless you have someone to corroborate all of this, someone like say the person who recorded all of this or runs the operation. Without that…."

I smiled ruefully. "That's the problem. He's dead and I kinda killed him. It was a fair fight, I swear, but things kinda just got out of control and you know…"

"Yes, I do know. Now you must go, before anybody knows you were here and I have to answer some very difficult questions one day at your trial. You need a live body, my friend, go find one. Meantime leave this all with me. I'll see what I can do about the journals. Maybe I know a few things, maybe not."

"Fine by me, just don't waste your life on it, I got other things on the go. If nothing comes of it just stick it somewhere safe, I'll be back for it all later."

"Absolutely, my friend."

It was my turn to smile wickedly. Hope wasn't dead yet, and neither was I.

So, that was that. I wasn't going anywhere fast, but at least it was in the right direction. I had enough evidence to get me elected King of this burned-out burg, or get me killed. Joey's advice made sense, someone still living to back me up was my best play, but they had to stay alive long enough. It was that impulse to shoot before being shot at that was always causing me grief. I didn't want to admit it but dying was how I stayed alive.

My office doorknob was almost within reach when a tiny fist gripped my left elbow, hard. I froze.

"Hey, where you bin. You owe me, mister," growled a familiar voice. Mrs Chen.

She snatched the wad I pulled out of my pocket, peeled off what I owed her, gave me that look, and shuffled back down the hall to her laundry. A tough little cookie that one, made grown men like me jump.

It felt good to be home, if only for a few minutes. Not that I missed the place, who would ever miss this rathole, but it was the only home I had. And no one had been in here, judging by all the dust heaped up on my desk. Joey had got me thinking. How were the two-legged sale items being brought in. They had to come in from somewhere and it figured they wouldn't be coming alone. If they were imports and not part of a domestic racket that meant something quick and quiet. If I could figure that out, maybe snatch one, I'd be halfway home.

My money was on train travel. Flying needed paperwork. Bus was too slow and had too many stops. This was a train town; two huge stations, acres of yard and more track than a spider's web. With instinct nudging me along, I figured to take another look at the stuff Lena had been so teary-eyed over. Maybe there was something in there now that made sense.

I tossed it all back on my desk, lit up a Dunhill for luck, and almost immediately came up with that something. It was a single sheet of tan paper, dated two weeks ago, PNR stationary with Stores Department Shipping Advice splashed across the top. We'd all looked at it and put it aside. Now it was front and centre.

It named a PNR Foreman, the Yard Section he was responsible for and a request for him to watch out for a specific rail car. Didn't mention where it was coming from, just a time, and to have it delivered to its usual spot in the Yard. Me, I didn't know a spur from a siding but I knew people who did. Better yet, I had an idea what that spot just might be. My fingertips began to tingle, this was something.

I hit the streets, dropped the last of my loose change at a news joint a couple blocks away. Grabbed every train schedule, plus any local paper with a schedule, pulled up a bench in a nearby park and got to it. There couldn't be that many trains in a day and with a time I shouldn't have any trouble finding what I was looking for.

What I needed was to link this car to a train, specifically one from the east. It would confirm the how and tell me positively where to look for the next who. I was getting closer to that all important live body, and peace for Addy. Not to mention getting my own skin out of the line of fire and back where it belonged, in the shadows. PI's don't do well in the light of day.

It was a sunny day but you wouldn't have known it by the dark cloud hanging over my bench. Papers went flying as I lost what little patience I had left. Nothing came even close and I had been through everything twice. That got me a sharp tap on my shoulder and a very loud "HEY" in my ear. I leaped to my feet, instinctively reaching for my old friend, until I caught sight of the blue uniform. I pulled my hand out slowly, clutching a pack of smokes.

"Look here, you," he admonished, waving his nightstick

under my nose.

"Yeah?"

"What do you think you're doing."

"Officer?" I didn't know what I was doing, unless hoping for the best counted.

"What on god's green earth do you think you're doing!"

"Just having a quiet little read is all, officer. Trying to keep up with things. You know how it is with the world these days."

"Ah, don't give me that, I seen what you bin up to and I've a good mind to take yuz in." He seemed genuinely peeved and I couldn't figure out for the life of me why. Clearly, he didn't know who I was or this would have gone a lot worse. Somehow my being parked on an innocent bench in a city park had him all tied up in knots.

"What for, I was just reading a paper. Last time I looked that wasn't an offence."

"Don't give me that, I hear it a hundred times a day. I could hear you from halfway across the park, I could, wailin' like a banshee and throwing things around like you was at home or something. Not on my beat, mister, not on my beat."

"Okay, okay, sorry," I growled. The temptation to do something I'd regret was caught in my throat, like bad shine on its way back up. I was close, I could just feel it and here was the law practically wiping his feet all over it.

"Okay, nothing, me old son. Look at this mess you've made. Littering, that's what it is, littering. A bloody big mess you've made and you expect to just walk away from it. Not on my watch, mister, not on my watch. Now you pick it all up, all of it. And mind your language, there's ladies hereabouts." And you wonder why I don't exactly have that respect for the uniform that I should. There's a murder a minute going on in this town and he's worried about a couple of lousy newspapers.

I shoulda kicked him where it hurts most but I almost kissed him instead. I'm down on my knees, with Moses watching over me while I cleaned up the Red Sea, when it came to me. The papers I had were todays, but I needed one from a week ago! And it just might be hiding in the trash can I was stuffing. The city fathers might have called themselves hard working, but not their lower paid brethren. This can was more than full and stank like hell. Soon as Moses harrumphed his approval of my efforts and moved on, I dumped it all out and tore through the mess. My link was soaked in coffee and glued to the bottom of the can.

What brought me to my knees on the sidewalk was some peekaboo work I did a couple of years back for some rich society dame. Hubby was suddenly never home and miss snooty wanted to know why. Tracked him down to a private railcar behind the PNR train station. Turned out the old geezer, a judge no less, was dancing it up with a couple of female friends, courtesy of a new friend. The girls kept him busy, enough to miss a court date or two, and a particular case got tossed. His new friend got some old friends back and miss snooty benched him for all he had.

Back then, my old friend Blackie Duff had laid it all out for me, how private railcars travelled across the country anywhere a train went. They travelled at the end of the train, in front of the caboose, for easier delivery once they reached their destination. This included the PNR yards which had one particular place to park them.

Peter might have been new in town but his journals had listed a lot of coded transactions. That suggested a lot of money was in play, enough to allow for more private forms of accommodation, and travel. What were the odds that Peter and his pals had their own private railcar and I knew where it was hiding? I couldn't smile hard enough.

Half an hour later I was lying on top of a boxcar, peering over the edge to see if X marked the spot. It did. There was just the one car, painted railroad brown, a single row of sash windows running the length, a platform at either end. The windows were curtained but little cracks of light still showed through. Someone was home.

After about an hour of swatting flies, some slick in a rumpled grey suit stepped out onto the rear platform and lit up. He looked around, didn't see anything he didn't like, and looked up at the stars. Took his time about it, like he was being paid by the puff.

That made it almost too easy. He lit up a second and then a

third, by which time I was close enough to smell his aftershave.
Dime store crap which your cheap hoods bathed in, like it gave them
some kind of in with the ladies, or protected them against the likes
of me. It didn't.

He continued to observe the moon until he suddenly saw
stars instead. Relieved him of his piece, dumped him off the
platform, and stepped into a dimly lit anteroom. Tried the two side
doors but they were locked, ahead was a third that was talking
quietly in its sleep. It murmured, so it wouldn't disturb the
neighbours. But all they would have heard was what my ear heard,
the clink of glasses and some gentle female chatter. And giggling.

Now came my favourite part of the job, quietly opening a
door in the face of who knows what. Could be anything from a
scream to a Thompson .45 with a full clip. And I've opened up on
both. But the real enemy in this situation is the door. Surprise
requires silence, and that's only if everything cooperates, especially
the hinges. A noisy hinge can be the difference between a quick
arrest and a quicker death.

Knowing my luck, this damn thing probably squeaked
enough to wake the dead. I took a deep breath, whipped it open and
stepped in, my .45 sweeping the room for trouble. What it found was
a beautifully appointed living room; couch, coffee tables, cushions,
brass lamps, the whole nine yards. The sides of the car were lined
with heavy drapes, the couch defended by two gorgeous girls armed
with champagne glasses, staring open mouthed at me.

At that moment, a door at the other end of the room swung
open and another grey suit stepped into the light, gun in hand. He
saw me, yanked out something snub-nosed, and fired twice, all in
the blink of an eye. I felt a slight flick as he holed the left side of
my jacket from the second round. I replied in kind, missing him
entirely. He chose not to tempt fate, vanishing the way he'd come,
leaving only a swirl of gun smoke behind. The girls continued to
stare, as if champagne was always accompanied by a gunfight.

We all held our breath, waiting for more company to come
charging out, but my luck held. A quick look out the other door
satisfied me we were still alone. I followed that up with a tour of a
bar in the far corner of the room and a shot of really good scotch. A

couple more of those and the shaking stopped. You never got used to this, no matter how many times you went through it. You breathe hard, sweat a lot, shake a little, who doesn't? Didn't mean I was good at it, just luckier.

The champagne tasters were a couple of heavily made up, lightly dressed cuties. Both had drinks in hand, glued to the couch and still breathing, my lucky day.

"Sorry about the noise, ladies. He wouldn't listen to reason so I had to get his attention." I turned my attention back to the scotch and read the label, Johnny Walker. Probably the best medicine I could think of for relaxing after a hard day's work. I poured myself another celebratory shot. I had what I'd come for, living, breathing evidence that some judge somewhere would appreciate. Addy would have been proud.

I leaned back against the bar, sipping my medicine. "You two got names?" I asked. Nothing. "Namu, namola, namini?" I growled. Still nothing. I thumped my empty shot glass against my chest. "Tony."

The taller of the two, a rangy brunette, put her drink down on a side table. Her face was pale despite the war paint.

"Anya." The lip was trembling a little. She gently elbowed the other in the ribs.

"Natalya." She with the bruised ribs and a blonde bob was positively shaking.

"Yeah, so, nice to meet ya. And no, I'm not going to shoot you. I just want to ask a couple questions is all." Silence.

"That's good. Drink?" I asked, waving the scotch bottle I was rapidly emptying.

The brunette was the brave one, wiggling her way over to me, glass in hand. Downed two full ounces without taking her eyes off me. I sighed inwardly. Of all the women in my life, it's the brunettes that have caused me the most grief. Not that I wish them any ill, but the browns of the world have done me no favours. Was it the colour?

"Tu parle Russki?" I asked in my best European.

"Da," was the answer I didn't want to hear. That was all the Russian I knew

Hand signals, a mouthful of English, a smattering of French, and an empty bottle got the party started. They cozied right up to me, all smiles and giggles, eager to pick up where they'd left off. They seemed convinced now I was the good guy, despite the gunplay. We played empty the bottle for a while and when the last drop spilled out it was time to go. Where to was Sandy's. I figured the girls could stay there for a while out of sight and hopefully out of mind. Lena would appreciate the company.

And that's when the cops showed up.

The back door of the car slammed open and two slick-haired gangsters in black boiler suits and stompers charged in. Railroad dicks, the last thing I needed. Aside from the danger of attracting any more of Constantine's boys, I'm always a little wary of railroad cops. Blackie Duff had warned me about them, a real tough bunch he said, don't cross them.

Blackie was an old rail hand who lived, ate, and breathed railway and coal dust. He held court deep within the rail yards and knew more about how things ran than the Foremen paid to run them. He was my go-to guy for all things rail related and on occasion kept me out of harm's way.

Railroads were privately run, which allowed them to man their own police force. They caught you on their property and they had every right to kick you where it hurt, a right they exercised frequently. The papers were continually full of stories about their welcoming attitude.

They had all the usual problems to deal with, stolen goods and equipment, runaways, stowaways, and the like. Trouble was the outside world had become a much darker and unforgiving place. Money was tight, dreams were gone, and work of any kind was not to be found. That left a lot of people looking, wherever they could for whatever there was. And they would get there any way they could, usually by rail.

There were so many extra passengers on freight trains all the railroad cops could do was direct traffic. Stop the train at the edge of town, clean everybody out, and then herd them over to the nearest highway. A long shuffle of desperate humanity looking for a way out, only there wasn't one. It wasn't a pretty sight.

There were two of them, and they stormed right in, waving nickel plated .38s around, yelling loud enough to wake the dead. What's going here, who fired those shots, who the hell are you, came snarling out. The girls replied with screams of outrage and indignation, mixed with a little fear. I finished my drink and put my hands up. I mean, even those peashooters could do some damage at close range, and club car range was close enough.

The shouting finally died down as our two new friends relaxed the show. The girls ended their noisy welcome just long enough to take a breath and then exploded in a blazing fury. They had drunk enough liquid courage to take on a bear, which is exactly what they did. Up came the hands, and slaps and kicks rained down on the two suits like angry hail. Seems that waving a gun in their faces had only made things worse. I made a mental note of that.

The one nearest to me, tall, pimply-faced and skinny, threw up his arms to keep the claws away from his face. His partner, shorter and stouter, returned fire with his own slaps and kicks, but that went nowhere. My two mighty hunters were very determined, very drunk, and went at it like a night at the fights.

It was all they could do not to get their tickets punched by a couple of drunken floozies. Skinny dropped his gun and sank to his knees, whimpering, hands covering his face. I picked up his gun and got back out of the way. His pal never stood a chance either. The moment he burst in and started yelling "Police. Stop where you are!" it was game on. With Skinny on the floor, it was game over.

Anya ended up sitting on the stout one like a jockey on an elephant, wailing away with both fists. Natalya was having her own time trying to wrestle his gun out of his hand. Suddenly successful, she crawled around trying to find a safe spot to aim from. I stepped over Skinny and yanked it out of her hands. It was getting to be too much. She didn't think so and gave me a look.

"Alright!" I yelled. "Alright, that's enough you two, break it up!" Natalya crawled over to the couch, a sour look on her big game hunter face.

"Get her off me! Get her off me!" came from the floor, loud and desperate. Anya continued to lay a beating on the elephant, complete with chapter and verse on how he'd scared her half to death, in Russian. I let it go, this was just too much fun

When she finally ran out of gas I called her quietly by name, nodding towards the couch. She slowly got to her feet, breathing heavily, still swearing at the elephant. He stayed put, arms across his face. A couple of swift kicks in the ribs and Anya flopped down on the couch beside Natalya. They were sweaty, breathing hard, and all smiles.

The war over, I deposited the guns in an empty ice bucket. Mine stayed where it was, watchful and available.

"Okay, so what gives," groused the Elephant, slowly getting to his feet. "Who the hell are you people? I oughta run you all in for trespassing and fighting. I'm an officer of the law, you know, I can do that."

"You and whose army," I quipped. "Seems like all you did was enter a private rail car unannounced, lose your guns, and get beat up by a couple of chippies. You two oughta be thanking me for pulling them off you, not trying to arrest anyone. You're lucky to be alive."

"Says you," said Elephants pal, getting up off the floor. "That don't change nuthin'. This here's private property and you're trespassing and we got every right to haul you all in."

"Drink?" I inquired in reply, pouring a couple fingers of something amber coloured into shot glasses I lined up on the bar. "Take my advice, next time talk nice to these wildcats. Guns only scare them and you see what happens when they get scared."

The two cops fished their heaters out of the bucket, put them back in their pockets nice and slow, and downed a shot glass each. I kept pouring, the girls kept staring, and life returned to normal.

"You boys got names?" I asked politely, pouring myself a double. After this little fracas I needed one. "Name's Ford, Tony Ford. I'm a PI. Allow me to introduce my associates. This one's Natalya and the one with the Joe Louis fists is Anya. They speak a whole lot of Russian, just a little English, and not much else."

"Okay, Ford." said Elephant. "Mind my askin' what you're all doin' in here? This is a private car. The owner don't like visitors much, which is why we come runnin' over when we heard the shots. We got special instructions from the Yard Boss."

"Do tell. I got my own boss. You boys wouldn't know Blackie Duff, by any chance? Friend of mine, lives around here somewhere. Never quite sure what he does for a living but he seems to think he runs the place."

"Duff?" asked Skinny. "Yeah, we know him. He's not the Yard Boss but he might as well be. Boss's name is Gardener, which is pretty much all he does all day, bastard, that and give us hell for any little thing. Say, got any more of this?" He slapped the shot glass down and I obliged with a nice long pour. Same for Elephant, we all became fast friends.

Long story short, the after-fight party became real merry. The girls worked their magic with winks and wiggles and had those two learning Russian in a heartbeat. Turns out Elephant's name was Stan, short for Stanislaus, single and a member of the local Ukrainian Relief association. That it wasn't Russian didn't seem to matter, just made him the hero of the hour. Someone from home the girls could talk to. Skinny's mom called him Albert.

The party progressed from boxing to dancing, my two heavy hitters lamenting loudly that Peter's musical taste was in his feet, all he had was opera.

"We want to dance," moaned Anya. "We sit too long on train, it move but we cannot, Peter say sit and have drink, you dance soon, but no dance. He say we go to pah-veel-ee-on where is big dance. Go by train, he take us and we dance, meet new people. They want marry us, make us good girls."

My ears perked up at that little commentary. This burned-out burg prided itself on a selfless devotion to the arts. They had operas, ballets, and recitals coming out of their rich and powerful ears. But more importantly, they loved to dance. Seemed like every corner in town had some kind of floor space devoted to sweaty bodies spinning like drunken tops to out of tune pianos.

"Natalya," I hissed quietly, pulling her aside. "You want to go dancing, that right?"

"Yes, we want dance. Peter promise."

"Yeah, I got that. Where? Did he say where?"

"Anya!" she bellowed. "Where we go dance? Where, where is dance, where is men?"

It took her a couple seconds to mull that over and then she blurted out the answer. Well, an answer.

"Beach! We go beach to dance!" Anya screamed.

Stan reacted sharply to that demand, nearly jumping out of his skin. His mile-wide smile died and he gave Al a look. Now he was all business, grabbing Al by the arm and steering him to the door. The girls threw both of them a look, unhappy as I was that the party was over. I tossed down my drink and slammed the glass on the bar.

"Hey, where are you two going," I grumbled. "Party's just getting started."

"Look, pal, we'd like to help you out but we gotta go. It's a busy night and a couple guys called in. We got a lot of ground to cover." Stan seemed a little nervous but I couldn't figure what about. He had a private car, two drunken chippies, and a bar full of booze. You'd have thought he'd be on his knees thanking me for the free party.

They beat it with me in hot pursuit.

"Listen you two, hold on a sec, willya, there's a couple things I need to know."

"Not from us you don't," replied Stan, shoving Al down the stairs. "We don't know nothing from nothing."

I grabbed Stan by the collar as he made his escape.

"Let go, you," he growled, straining at the leash. Weren't these two in a hurry? Was it something I'd said? I tightened my grip on his collar.

"Yeah," barked Al, "Let him go. We don't want no trouble." He was fumbling around in his suit and then flashed his piece, all casual like, so I could see he meant business. An amateur playing pro. Pointing it at me would have been a bad idea.

I threw my hands up in mock surrender. "Okay, okay, I get it, you got work to do. Look, at least do me a favour, find Blackie, tell him I gotta see him."

Yeah, sure thing, was all I got as they quickly staggered off into the night. It was late, and I didn't think Blackie would show, but this beach pavilion thing was ringing in my ears. It had certainly taken Stan's attention away from Anya and I had to wonder why.

Constantine was trading in people, no question, a sleazy little enterprise that probably made him buckets of money. And produced lots of misery. But it wasn't the kind of thing you wanted to broadcast all over town. This was back room, behind closed doors stuff. When you trade in souls the last thing the devil wants is any kind of attention. It would fit Constantine's style, flash and cash, but all the same, why tell the whole world what you're up to.

I might have been too drunk to think things through any further, but thanks to Anya I had a choice to make. If I hid the girls at Sandy's this link in the chain might disappear and I'd be no further ahead. Sobering them up and shaking what I needed out of them might clear things up a little, but that would take time. And that I didn't have. The longer we stayed put the sooner somebody else might find us, and I was running out of bullets.

I puffed my way through a couple of smokes on the platform out back, enjoying the cool of the evening and the relative quiet of a rail yard putting itself to bed. Didn't seem right somehow, two steps forward two steps back, still in the same pickle, even with the girls. If this was somebody's idea of a joke I wasn't laughing. My old gran wouldn't have questioned it, god's will she would have said, it's all part of his grand plan. Grand plan or not I wasn't having any of it. I wanted this thing done with and the sooner the better. Time was money, you didn't make any doing time.

CHAPTER TEN

Back in the train car, the girls had settled in for the night, shoes off, stretched out together on the couch. I was pouring a nightcap into a highball glass when a bomb went off outside the car. One minute I was wishing the last drops into the glass, the next I'm on the floor with the glass and its contents all over me. Something had walloped the car, sending everything flying. I was on my feet in a flash, gun out, ready for anything. Nothing. Then the car jerked and we were moving.

Leaving my two beauties to sleep it off, I yanked the back door open and stepped out onto the small platform. Damn near fell off as the car took another jolt, picking up even more speed. A train whistle sounded, long and loud. We were getting a free ride to somewhere. Blackie.

What those two idiots had told him I could only guess, but he'd moved fast enough. If this was another part of the plan it wasn't doing me any favours. I needed to be in town, putting this thing to bed. I finished my smoke and flung the butt at the passing rails in disgust. For one mad moment I thought about following it and hoofing it back to town. But that would mean abandoning my two alibis.

We sailed passed endless rows of crappy wooden fences and beat-up shantys no self-respecting dog would slum in. The air was hot and humid, the dampness sticking to my shirt like a thirsty barfly. There was just a hint of coal smoke in the evening air mixed with the thick smell of the world beyond the tracks.

So, where were we going? What message was Blackie sending that I was too angry, and too drunk, to see? I went on a tour to see who else was going on this little jaunt with us. The first car I eased into answered that question. It was jammed to the rafters with a very loud collection of the city's middle and lower classes. Men and women, all dressed to the nines, all yapping away at full throttle. I was about to grab the nearest bowtie and drag him out the back of the car, when a conductor appeared.

He took one look at me and said the words I was dreading. "Tickct plcasc."

"Yeah, listen. About that. I don't exactly have one. See, I was just …"

He was horrified. "No ticket!" he gasped. "No ticket? Where did you get on, what station? What do you mean by this! I'll have to see you off!"

"No, look, I'm in the car back there, and we just got up when the train started moving. We haven't had time to …"

"Oh in that case, no need!" he snorted, relieved. "No need. That's a private car, sir, and if you come from there you don't need a ticket. Nosiree! Just make sure you stay in there or I will have to sell you one. Are you going all the way, sir? I was informed we were taking on another car but not who or what. Are you going to the end of the line, sir?"

"Depends. Exactly where is all the way."

He ticked the points off on his fingertips like it was some kind of test he was trying to pass. "Hayes Junction through to Lansing, then past Grand Junction to Alberton and last stop at Patterson. We stop there for fuel and water, turn around, and start back at one in the morning."

"Patterson, eh? Remind me what's up there, would ya. I'm kinda new in town and the girls, I mean my friends, are taking forty winks before we get there."

"I'm not surprised, they'll need all their energy and in very short order. Patterson Station just happens to the largest outdoor dance pavilion in a hundred miles. I know Altec keeps claiming it's bigger, but that's only because they count the train station platform. They can't do that it's railway property and not for the public to use as a dance hall."

"A dance pavilion, eh, sounds about right. The girls kept talking about wanting to go dancing, so I guess that would be the place."

"Yes sir, it would, now if you'll excuse me I've got two more cars to go through before we pass Grand Junction. It's very tiresome and I'm short a man but I've got to finish. I've just got to."

I looked at him puzzled. "Why is that, if you don't mind my asking?"

"Tickets!" he snapped. "Everyone has to have a ticket

otherwise they get put off, and the last station to do that is Grand Junction. It's the rules, sir, company rules."

"I'll keep that in mind. Thanks, pal." But he was gone, pushing his way through a sea of sweaty bodies swaying to the rhythm of a train at full speed. I retreated back to the car, dropped into an armchair and tried to grab a few winks myself.

I don't pretend to be a light sleeper, I could snore through a hurricane given the right liquid incentive. Even so, you learn to sense change when it happens, no matter how slight. Some days that's all the warning you're gonna get, you learn to get a feel for it. That's what got me up in a hurry, the train was slowing down.

Stiff didn't begin to describe how I felt. Armchairs weren't as comfortable as they looked. I dragged myself over to the nearest window, slammed it open, and stuck my head out. The cool night air felt good on my face, and so did the sight of the upcoming train station. Patterson Station said a passing sign. So, we were going dancing.

The window beside me came alive as two eager dancers took in the same view. Squeals of delight and then they were back inside, standing in front of a big mirror opposite the couch, trying to make themselves pretty. I thought I had it bad just trying to stay on my feet, but they were trying to slap on some war paint. We started to slow down as a series of whistle blasts announced that we had arrived at Patterson station.

Hundreds of dance patrons poured off the cars until the train station was filled to bursting. It was a mob scene, a noisy, jostling, sea of humanity talking and laughing like it was Christmas and they getting off at the North Pole. I could see nothing and no one that seemed interested in the car or my alibis but, given the crowd, that wasn't surprising.

Two eager faces exploded in squeals of delight as they viewed it all from the window. That was enough for them, and it was all I could do to keep them from running off into the night. They shot me the kind of looks that would have killed lesser men but I insisted.

"You can't go and that's final, it's too dangerous. Like I been telling you, this ain't a safe place. There's bad people out there looking for you." There was an angry silence. They didn't believe me. I was supposed to be the good guy here, not the warden assigning cells. I made with a winning smile and tried again.

"You sure you don't know why you're here, or who's supposed to meet you?"

The long faces told me I'd made a fool of myself, and two mortal enemies. I sighed heavily, shaking my head. Somebody had gone to a lot of trouble to snatch us and the car and drag us all this way. That suggested a welcoming committee, probably a couple of grey-haired sugar daddies coming to claim their prizes. Throw a little scare into them, get a couple of names, and I'd be sitting pretty. Money didn't like publicity.

But my two friends didn't understand this. All they could see, and hear, was the good times ahead. They didn't understand that it came with its own danger, a danger I was trying to steer them clear of. Yeah, I get it, not every case is cut and dried, but this was like trying to chase a cat with a can tied to its tail. Every time I got close enough to grab it, something would spook it and we'd be back to square one. It was tempting just to shoot it and be done with it, but another body I didn't need.

And then they bolted for the front door.

"Hey you two, get back here!"

But they were already scrambling into the corridor and freedom. I cursed loudly and tore after them, wishing I'd tried another approach, like handcuffs. A short-lived run, they met up with company soon as they stepped on the platform. And not a couple of well-heeled gents in pinstripes, but a couple of gorillas in cheap suits. The girls froze in their tracks.

"Hello girls," said a size 42 with narrow shoulders, looking them over. "Been hoping to meet up with youse. I'm Ted and this here's Fred. Why don't you two come along with us, we've got someone real anxious to meet youse." He backed his suit coat off his right hip to show a flash of chrome plating.

"No, no, we not going," Natalya protested, shrinking away from him. Me, I hung back inside the doorway, listening to all this, ready to step in

"Yeah, yeah, come on let's go, honey, I ain't got all night."

He made a grab for her arm. She shrank away as if he had leprosy or something.

Anya stepped in front of her friend and pushed at the arm. This rapidly became a game of keep away, but Ted and Fred weren't in the mood. Fred gave Ted a look and made to pull out his piece but he wasn't fast enough. With the crowd so close, the girls simply turned and vanished into it. Ted gave his pal that now what do we do look, and followed by Fred, pushed in after them.

I stepped down onto the ground, not sure what to do myself. One second everything's in place the next I'm empty handed. I lit a smoke and took a couple puffs while I steeled myself for this. I'm not a big fan of crowds and I didn't like the odds of finding any of them again, but what other choice was there. I could only hope the girls were smart enough to dodge the trouble that was coming after them. I ditched my smoke and waded into the crowd.

Crowds can be a PI's best friend, they just take getting used to. Hanging back lets you see but not be seen, follow but not be followed. The trick was to maintain enough distance to react quickly or duck out of the way. Trailing these two idiots was almost too easy. They had come to a party dressed for a funeral, marking them like flies floating in beer.

I let the partygoers lead the way, taking station behind a group of half-dressed babes and their bow-tied escorts. We moved at a good pace, past the station and onto a boardwalk, lit at intervals by Chinese lanterns hung from poles, and surrounded by a pine forest. We were a long, noisy, snake of humanity, shuffling purposefully along without a care in the world.

Keeping Ted and Fred in sight was easy enough. They kept jumping up and down like they had ants in their pants, trying to get a look ahead and somehow spot the girls. Like they had any chance in this crush. Which worked just fine for me until the crowd got them turned around, and they jumped up and spotted me. Maybe it was the eye contact, maybe they recognised me from somewhere, but the second they saw me the chase was on.

The one grabbed the other by the shoulder, pointed in my direction and yelled in his ear. He nodded and the two of them pushed their way out of the crowd, and vanished into the trees. I followed, racing up to where they'd disappeared before taking the plunge myself. I wasn't used to playing in the woods but you go where you gotta. I hauled out my piece, chambered a round, and went straight in. If we were going to play in the woods, I wanted to get in the first shot.

Muffled curses up ahead told me someone else was having difficulty fighting off the pine cones. I charged into the darkness, following words of encouragement not meant for me. In a chase like this, you go in hard and fast, finger on the trigger. Odds are they'll see you coming long before you see them.

The voices stopped a short time later but I kept going. The sand underfoot made for slow going but muffled my footsteps. Then I hit an upslope and went flat on my face in the undergrowth. I swore loudly, spitting out sand and pine needles. That caught someone's ear, and a shot whizzed overhead. Then a second shot, followed by loud, nervous, voices that faded slowly away.

I crawled over a small sand dune, peering carefully over the top. They were maybe fifty feet away, backpedalling down a long strip of sandy beach, sweeping the area with their pistols. The boom from my .45, coming as it did from out of nowhere, was enough to turn them around and start them running again. I stood up and gave chase.

This was a new one for me, hunting a couple of hired guns along a beach at midnight. We could barely see each other but that didn't stop us from trading shots. I hadn't done any night fighting for quite some time but the old lessons hadn't left. Aim, shoot, dodge right, drop. The only difference was nothing heavier was coming back in reply to shower me with dirt and scraps of iron.

This went on until they vanished into the darkness. I gasped to a halt and grabbed at my ribs, tried to keep my chest from exploding. You've never felt pain until you've tried to cough up a lung and tasted the bitter results. As I sucked in the cool night air I had to ask myself if Sandy was right. I shouldn't be this dead on my feet, was I getting too old for this? She seemed to think so, but when did I ever listen to advice.

Soon as I could breathe without spitting fire I holstered my piece and splashed some lake water on my face. This whole thing was moving at speed, going in more directions than a compass and leaving me a little lost. I didn't like that not being in charge, not knowing what to do next or where to go. I prided myself on being able to bloodhound a trail, make sense out of nonsense. That I couldn't this time got me more determined.

That I was relentless, stubborn, and nobody's friend, was nothing new. That came from how many years of eating German dirt and dodging the grim one. There was just something about this PI business that had grabbed me by the lapels and wouldn't let go. I knew I couldn't change the world, all I could do was tend to my little corner of it and make the bad guys in it pay.

Even as I trudged along the lake's edge, I could hear the faint sounds of merriment up ahead. After what seemed like forever, the sound of a dance band and a large crowd dancing it up put me back on the trail. The Pavilion turned out to be a massive barn like structure not fifty yards from the lake, surrounded by any number of smaller open air stalls, selling everything from indigestion tablets to corn dogs and corn liquor. And all of it lit up like it was Christmas.

The roar of the crowd sucked me in, sat me at a table, and put a chipped glass of mother's best firewater in my hands. This wasn't her best parlour stuff, but it mixed well with smokes and a couple of greasy dogs. A short time later I was ready to start trolling the crowd for any familiar faces, male or female.

Well, that was the idea, but there had to be over a thousand people running around the joint, yelling and screaming and having a high old time. The music was loud enough to wake the dead and deafen the living, and trolling the side-lines annoying all the wallflowers didn't get me anywhere fast.

I pushed my way through the mob like an angry bull in a sweaty china shop, looking for any signs of anybody. Nothing, they were all of them gone. All I got for my efforts were bruised shoulders and a lot of vacant looks when I asked anything. They were all so wrapped up in having a good time I could have shot someone and no one would have noticed. Fine, they didn't want to be found, I got that, but that put me right back to square one, again. I didn't know if I should laugh, cry, or just shoot something.

I'd never seen this many people in one place, not since the

end of the big one. A lot of guys went through a lot of very bad things to make sure this party got started, so I hoped to hell they were enjoying it. If the lights ever went out again, I'm not so sure too many of us would volunteer to turn them back on again.

I ran across some old soldier scrounging through the garbage a stone's throw from the party. He was wearing a familiar army green jacket, had somebody's leftovers in his hands, and a hunted look about him. He jumped about a foot when I tapped him on the shoulder, waiting for a blow that never came.

"So what's your story," I growled. "Got nothing better to do than steal stuff?"

"Who me sir, no sir, just hungry sir." he replied. "Just an old doughboy down on his luck a little."

"That so? Where."

He straightened up a little and tried to look me in the eye. Best those old bones could do was my collar. "Three years in France, all of it up to my ass in mud and guts."

I'd heard that story before, and from better men than him, but he was still paying the price of being forgotten. I took his dinner out of his hands, tossed it back into the garbage, lit up a pair of smokes and gave him one. He jammed it into his lips, drawing a first puff that ended halfway down the stick. A coupla coughs and hunted turned happy.

I sat him down at a table beside a stall selling corndogs and whistled up enough grub to last him a week. It vanished as quickly as he could inhale it, filling a belly that probably hadn't been full for months. I indulged myself and we ate in silence, mentally sharing those moments that all soldiers do, hell on earth, lost friends, and survival.

For desert, we shared a pint of mother's milk and more Luckies, while I quizzed him on the train situation. Where they were from here and how soon they left. I'd decided to go back to town to see what I could salvage from this mess. And that's all this was, a giant pain-in-the-ass mess that had me maybe doing a stretch for nothing more than being the guy who found a body in an alley and asked a question.

The trains were just through the trees he said, savouring the sweet scent of a good smoke. Just follow that path yonder for a hundred yards or so and you'll find the station right in front of you. Trail is lit up so even a blind man can find his way. I stuffed the rest of my Luckies into his shirt pocket along with a twenty and sent him on his way. They can't all be forgotten.

The car was right where I'd left it, quietly occupying a siding close to the station where we'd first pulled up. The engine was at rest, quietly puffing away to keep up steam while the engineers crawled lovingly all over it with oily rags. That was something I'd never been able to get my head around, grown men playing with trains like they were a second wife or good bookie. My pal Blackie Duff lived that life in the PNR yards in town, no life like it he would say. Free food, free house, no cops, what else could a guy ask for.

Nobody was home so I stretched out on the couch, still fresh with the scent of its last occupants. I hadn't expected the girls to be here but knowing those two, they already had their arms around a couple of swells who'd treat them nice and give them a good home. At least I hoped so, it wasn't something I could have given them even if I'd found them. As for the suits, well, they'd turn up somewhere, bad pennies always do. Just look at me.

The train rattled back into town during the early dawn, crashed to a halt right where we'd started, and deposited the living dead onto a platform out back of the PNR station. Not until the engine whistled long and low, chugging off into the dawn, did I come to life. The other long low moan heard was me trying to sit up. I was covered in cigarette ash and butts, and couldn't remember much more than my name, and where I thought I might be.

Getting up onto my feet was slow and painful, stumbling around in the dark trying to get my bearings, and my brain working. I lurched into Constantine's private bathroom and said hello to the sink for a few minutes. Would have cleaned up but couldn't figure out the taps. Cursed my way back out and over to the bar, looking for something, anything, liquid I could hose myself down with.

Found a case of soda water and went to work. I've washed in worse so something bottled could only be good, right? The bottles were still sealed and I could see through them but why that was important I didn't know. My brain was still out cold and what was left of me was going from memory until it came to. Added ice to the water, that'll wake you up like nothing else.

A slow shave with a really expensive razor, a splash of something very flowery across the chops and I was starting to feel human again. And didn't I look the picture of health. Either that or the mirror was as beat up as I felt. Whatever else I might have thought about the guy, Constantine did travel in style. His shirts were silk and a bit tight across the chest but he didn't need them anymore. Same with his ties.

Dressed and pressed, I relit one of the longer butts left on the bar and stepped out of the back of the car. The sun was already up and shining brightly, promising another long day of heavy heat and short tempers. All it promised me was the prospect of a room at the crowbar hotel. As if I didn't have enough to deal with, losing all my witnesses, one dead boss man, and a very thin set of circumstances. All I did was trip over a dead woman, and now I was wanted, dead or dead.

What had me thinking was all this running around. Was it just my imagination or did anybody really not care about what was going on? There were bodies and bullets flying everywhere yet nobody seemed to have noticed. I should have been in irons a long time ago, pleading for my life with the legal eagles downtown, and yet not a peep out of anyone.

Constantine's boys didn't seem to be too concerned. It looked like business as usual, so was somebody else running things? That would make sense, but the question was who. And why. Running illegals into the country was nothing new, false paperwork was par for the course, so what made all this so different. Somebody had to know something and I still had to find that someone, if only for my own satisfaction, and freedom.

More importantly, I was dying for a real cigarette and something to swallow besides fresh air. The station was open for business, like it ever really closed, and the joint was jumping. A noisy sea of humanity rushed back and forth like they were trying to book passage on the Ark and only two seats left. Grabbed some kid dragging a pile of the latest edition across the waters, gave him a deuce and sent him off for supplies while I got a shine.

Junior came rocketing back in a hot minute with a couple packs of Luckies and a mickey of good enough Scotch. He was smart enough to hand me the goods first then pocket the change. Popped a couple of his own sticks, lit them and passed me one, but not the coinage. Smart kid.

As I sat there, from off in the back of the foyer a wildly waving hand caught my eye. Anya, and right beside her Natalya, the two of them arm-in-arm with Stan and Albert, the railway flatties. I jumped up, thinking more trouble was in the works but the crowd swallowed them up and they were gone. I took a few steps in their direction but they had just up and disappeared. I swore loudly and threw away a perfectly good cigarette in disgust.

Those two would be okay, I reasoned, they were survivors and they had their hooks into two gents who would probably fall all over themselves to stay on their good side. Fine for them but they were my last two hopes for a quick end to this business.

It crossed my mind that I'd had some success at Constantine's warehouse; it might be an idea to give it another quick look-see. After last night's escapades somebody had to be having second thoughts. Every time they turned around bad penny me was right behind them, getting closer.

Woke up a cabbie, tossed him some silver, and jumped out a block away so I could sniff the wind first. From there I could see that the warehouse doors were wide open and nothing was moving. I swore under my breath and hurried on over to take a closer look.

I entered more than a little angry with myself. This thing was getting further and further away from me and I was better than that. I could argue that I really wasn't really on a case, that no one was waiting for my report and professional insight, but I would be arguing with myself. Meantime, I was climbing the top ten list downtown with no way of getting off.

There was a black Ford sedan idling inside, trunk open, and a wave of dark hair sitting in the back seat. Farther in, two gents were busy dragging an overly large suitcase across the cement floor towards the car. Looks like I'd caught two rats leaving the ship and they hadn't invited me along for the trip. They were taking somebody else.

CHAPTER ELEVEN

The big one with a shock of red hair and suspenders saw me first.

"Little early, ain't ya copper, thought you guys were told to hold off until noon. Everybody's gone and you ain't getting paid 'til later."

"I can wait," I replied quickly.

The lugging stopped at this point, directly in front of me and not a short stone's throw away. Red's companion, a short little plug-ugly with a broken nose, was all out of breath and hunched over, trying to get it back. Red was a cool one, lighting the stub of a thick cigar without taking his eyes off me.

"Well, it's gonna be a while, buddy, the new man said there's too much heat on us. Ain't nobody getting nothing until we're all set up in the new place."

It wasn't the sunlight making me sweat I had the two of them dead to rights and my gun was buttoned up tight under my left armpit. Yeah, I know, clothes make the man but I didn't want to be buried in them today. They weren't my clothes.

"And what new place is that," I asked innocently. "No one said anything to me about that. You got an address or something? Might be I want to go see the new man and introduce myself."

"Is that a fact? You new here? What'd you say your name was?" Red was suddenly very curious and I didn't have any more answers for him. I kept talking, thinking maybe things might smooth over if I kept it up long enough.

"Didn't say. I was just walking by saw the doors open and figured I'd drop in and say hi."

"Oh, did you now. And what station are you from again?" His hands were hard on his hips, his nose in my face. He didn't believe me either.

"Didn't say."

"You aren't for saying much, are you, copper."

"Nope."

That did it. We parted company, they drew their pieces and snapped off a couple of shots smooth as silk. Me, I stepped

sideways, madly going for mine. We traded quick shots while I slid into the shadows. Bullets flew back and forth without much more damage than chipped concrete and splintered wood. I wondered if maybe they were as hungover as I was.
They retreated farther into the warehouse, firing quickly until loud clicks replaced the crack of gunfire. Footsteps faded quickly as they beat it out the back way.

That left the suitcase and the dark hair, neither of which had moved.

I was almost afraid to look. I was hoping whoever was in the car was more of my missing evidence, so long as she wasn't full of holes. I peered in a side window, just to be sure I wasn't dreaming. She was there alright, another dame, mid-thirties, hands folded in her lap, making like she was part of the furniture.

I tapped a knuckle on the glass and she turned to face me, big brown eyes absolutely bursting with fear. I gave her my best I don't shoot women smile and eased the back door open, taking care not to take my eyes off of hers. You just never knew.

"Hi, I'm. Tony. You got a name, doll, you alright?" She nodded quickly. A thick accent said hello back, that her name was Georgiana.

"Look, honey, um, I'm not going to hurt you, understand? I'm not with them," I said, nodding in the direction of her two departed friends.

"Is good," she replied tartly. "I not like them. Where we go?"

That was a good question, where were we going to go?

I told her not to move and went over to grab the suitcase. Whoever packed it had made sure it was full as it could get. It took all I had to drag it over to the trunk and dump it in. The back end bounced a little when I slammed the trunk closed. Time to play chauffeur.

There was crap all over the front seat, cigarette butts, stale dogs and empty beer bottles. I shoveled it all aside and slid into the driver's seat. The car slid easily into gear and we were off, my newest alibi parked in the back like she was the Queen of Sheba. She didn't move a muscle or say another word but the few she had spoken got me to thinking. I'd heard that voice before somewhere.

Several blocks later my brain kicked in and reminded me that Lena spoke like that, legs out to here Lena. Night Butterfly Lena. And didn't I think I had another one in the back seat? Probably. And didn't I think she knew everything? Probably. And didn't I think she was going to be my ticket to freedom? Maybe. I mean, how likely was she to spill the beans without a good reason? I figured she had every reason not to.

Going to the authorities with what she knew wouldn't be easy. She'd be out in the open with a pretty big target on her back, even with me as her bodyguard. Last time out had paid well but I hadn't enjoyed all that fetching and carrying. She was blond and beautiful and a right royal pain in the ass.

Daddy Warbucks had been doing some really bad things with some really bad characters, until one of them broke ranks and ratted him out. DW needed his darling princess protected while he spilled it to the Badges downtown. The work wasn't my usual line but I couldn't pass up the prospect of some easy money.

It's bad enough that you're on call and constantly looking over your shoulder. Add to that a whiny princess, a yappy dog, and an insatiable thirst for the nightlife, and it was a month that remains a blur. Yeah, I delivered her safe and sound, but to daddy's funeral and not into his loving arms. They couldn't get to her so they got him, with a full clip from a Thompson.

She inherited it all, the mansion, the servants, the legit half of daddy's empire and more cash than most banks. Last I heard she was living it up at her newest venture, some sleazy nightclub downtown with an equally sleazy boyfriend slash owner. And a very drunk little dog. I had a better idea.

Mid-morning should have meant a traffic stopping display of arms and legs sunning themselves all around Sandy's place. Turns out today was housework day. We walked into a cloud of dust and curses and wiggling bottoms that would have made a sailor blush. The girls were giving their home sweet home the once over twice, if I understood half of what I was hearing. Not the kind of housekeeping I was used to but it produced the faintest hint of a smile on Georgiana's lips.

We made our way through the heaped-up furniture and rolled up carpets, to where the cigarette smoke was thickest and the curses loudest, the kitchen. And even in there the pace was frantic. It was a sea of glass and china, half-dressed girls up to their armpits in soap suds and damp shorts. I wondered if they hired out.

The red-haired shorts turned around.

"Hey there, handsome, long time no see. So, who's your friend," Sandy yelled over the giggling and squealing.

"No one you'd know," I said, "Just someone I found in the back of a car."

"No kidding, musta been some car."

"Yeah, you might say that. Listen, you got someplace quiet, I need Lena."

"Lena?"

"Yeah," I said, nodding at my new friend. "I'm thinking they might know each other and I gotta know what she knows, and soon."

Sandy gave me that who do you think you're kidding look and led us out back.

The back yard was not bigger than a postage stamp, fenced on three sides with a gate at the far end. The alley beyond that saw more late night traffic than most night clubs. There was even a flatfoot out there, to keep things moving, so to speak. Is that why we paid taxes? What would the good citizens of this burg think of the entertainment their illustrious leaders were shelling out for?

Today they were getting a break from all that sweat and toil, the yard full of sheets, pillowcases and other interesting items, enjoying a stiff midday breeze. That left us to conduct our business with our backs to the wall just outside the back door. And as it happened out of that sea of shame strolled Lena, long legs and all, holding an apron full of clothes pegs.

She stopped dead in her tracks when she saw my companion. The moment of truth. I watched as those big brown saucers toured Georgiana from nose to toes, a little flicker to the left eyebrow. She walked right up to her, words I didn't understand came out, and lots of them.

Georgiana came to life like she'd been electrocuted, bursting into song herself. The two of them went at it like a couple of circus hucksters, tongues flapping and arms waving. They went at it so hard I thought their lips might explode. I didn't speak the lingo, but no seemed to be a pretty common word in any language. Lena was throwing it at Georgiana like the bases were loaded in a tie game.

There were only so many pitches she could take before Georgie finally buried her face in her hands and burst into tears. That got Lena going, next thing you know the two of them were arm in arm, having some kind of crying party. I looked at Sandy, eyebrows raised.

Sandy pulled me aside.

"What gives," I asked. "Those two really know each other? I was just kidding."

"I don't know, I mean I don't speak Russian. Lena's kind of a loner so I don't know that much about her. But she sure knows your friend."

"I was kinda hoping that might be the case. Listen, any chance you can hide her for a while? I need her out of the way but available. She might be just what the doctor ordered, at least for me anyways."

"Hey, don't get any ideas about her. She's not your style, just look at her."

"I am looking, that's just the thing. She's looking like the only living thing I've got to get me out of the jam I'm in."

"Again? Oh, honey, you need another line of work."

"Like that's gonna happen. Listen, do me this favor, would ya? I need to keep her out of sight for a while. There's gonna be a whole a lot of bad guys tearing up this town looking for her and I need her alive."

She sighed. "Okay, I'll see what I can do. Just leave her with me but don't come around for a couple of days, this may take some doing."

"Thanks doll."

"Yeah. You owe me for this, again." Like she had any chance of collecting.

The sedan was easier to deal with. I stuck to my deal with Stinger and took my stolen business elsewhere. Drove it around the corner and parked it in the first public parking lot I could find. It would sit there and rust all to hell before anybody noticed. I was tempted to tell the kid who gave me the ticket what he could do with it, but why tempt fate. It would be the one time I'm generous with somebody else's wheels and it comes back to bite me.

I swept the car for anything of interest before I said goodbye. The stuff in the trunk could wait a little but I liked to be thorough. I've solved more cases with stuff I've found under the seat than you might think. Out of sight doesn't mean out of mind, especially when I'm the one frisking the car.

That's how I came up with the notebook, a small leather notebook, the kind you could pick up at any five and dime. It was filled with page after page of numbers and letters, a kind of shorthand that made little sense to me. At the back, of the book two more pages of numbers, in no particular order, with more of the same shorthand. They might have identified something or someone, but I was pretty sure it was a someone. I knew local telephone numbers when I saw them, and these sure as hell were.

First Georgiana, and now this, I was finally starting to see a little daylight. Guess Lady Luck had seen enough and decided to throw me a bone or two. I had my live body, and now a little something more, if I could figure out what the code was. Making a couple of random calls might shake something loose.

Pick a number, any number, belched Kelly at some long ago lunch date. Pester, bother, annoy, until they say something to make you go away. Why do you think I'm such a success, he roared, throwing wide his arms, why do you think I own all this! Get a body all riled up and they'll say anything to make it stop, anything! Usually it's the wrong anything and then you've got them! Then they really will do anything you want to make it stop.

I didn't have his gift of gab but I did share in his persistence. I'd pulled my own version of this a couple of times, complete with a liquid throat soother in between calls. Call a guy enough times, and yeah, something stupid comes out, mixed in with the usual threats to life and limb. You've got nothing but they think you've got something and they'll pay anything to find out what it is, or to make you go away.

That's all I got for the first three or four numbers, a whole lot of stupid, but no one dumb to say who it was at the other end. Call number five was different. The voice at the other end gave me a deep, gravelly, yeah whadda ya want? It took a few seconds to sink in but I recognized the voice.

"Stella?"

"Yeah, who's this, whadda ya want?"

"It's Ford."

"Ford? What the hell are you doing on this line! Get off, it's private!"

"Just doing my job. And just what the hell are you doing with a private line?"

"Never you mind, where the hell are you?"

"Never you mind, I'm working. Now, about this line."

"Stuff that! Drop what you're doing and get your butt over here right now!"

"What for?" I asked innocently. I couldn't hide the smile, the one person I had counted out was the one I could now count on. The light of day was getting a whole lot brighter.

"Don't argue with me, buster, just do it," she growled. "And don't tell nobody about this, okay? Just you and me, Tony, just you and me."

Well, that was a new one, her calling me Tony. I never got more than a hey you out of her, so, what kind of gold was this I had in my hands.

It was long towards dinnertime when I answered the summons and pushed my way through the crowd. Lit up a smoke and went looking for an open booth. There were plenty, which spoke to the quality of the dinner menu. I counted myself a happy customer but I only had one favorite and it wasn't even on the menu. Did that make me someone special? She didn't think so, especially since I couldn't pay up half the time.

"Listen buddy, we're closing early, so make it something quick," said a welcoming voice from behind the counter. Then that happy face of hers, cigar and all, peered through the hatch and saw who it was.

"Oh, it's you, about time you got here."

"Glad to see you too, sunshine." I casually flipped open a menu and pretended to read it. She struggled to shove her bulk into the bench seat opposite me.

"So, what's so important I gotta drop everything to come and see you? Your ex back in town again? I told ya before, he's still running."

"Yeah, yeah, listen. Word is a lot of things been happening lately and you're right in it."

"Nothing new in that. You keeping tabs on me or something?"

"Not exactly. And it don't matter anyhow. You get onto something and you're harder to follow than a rabbit with the runs. I just hear things, is all. So, talk at me, where did you get that number from?"

I put down the menu and lit up another smoke. She was trying to stare me down which meant I had something hotter than hot in my pocket.

"Why do you want to know, what's it to you?" I sent a smoke ring skyward.

"Plenty. And I'm not the only one. I got people want to hear what you know."

"Yeah, well, they can hear this. I've been chasing everyone, and everything, for the last couple days and getting nowhere fast and I'm done with that. She was dead when I found her, I asked around a little, then some character named Constantine starts giving me the gears. I don't know exactly who he is but I got a pretty good idea, only he ain't around anymore."

She leaned forward, a look on her face like she was trying to stare me to death. "You know him, he say anything?"

"Nah, he wasn't talking much last time we met. All I got to show for it is this," I said, pulling out the notebook and thumbing idly through the pages. I thought her eyes would pop out of that thick skull of hers. "I got no idea what all this means, if it means anything at all, but I got people who can find out for me. It stays with me until I get some answers from someone, anyone, even you."

She stuck out her meat hook of a right hand, and waved like she was inviting me into the principal's office.

"Gimme."

"Can't do that," I said.

"Why not."

"I need it."

"No, you don't."

"Yeah, I do. In case you hadn't noticed I got more trouble hanging around my neck than a string of pearls. Way I see it, this just might be my ticket out, so no dice."

"You don't know what you got there, I do, so gimme!"

"Not going to happen," I said leaning forward and scowling back.

"Freddie!" she roared, her eyes not leaving mine.

"Yas'm?"

"Feed the man, anything he wants, on the house. And get him some of the good stuff."

I sat back, and pulled out another smoke, trying to buy a little time. This was a woman who wouldn't sell a crumb to a starving rat, present company excepted. I'd seen her upset before but not like this. Truth be told, if there was anyone I really trusted it was her. We had a long history, her and me, so it took only two deep draws to decide.

I slapped the notebook into her open palm and sat back, heart pounding. She was up and gone, don't move her only comment.

A short time later my usual slammed down in front of me, sizzling hot and heaped high. I only ever wanted one thing and while she constantly tossed things like liver and meatloaf at me, I held my ground. The steak sizzled, the fries snapped, the gravy thick enough to pave a road. The good stuff was a full mickey of imported hooch, single malt, and good enough to come with its own glass. So good in fact, that Freddie took a moment to wipe the glass with a corner of his apron.

I heard a phone go into use somewhere in the back, probably the one I'd called her on, and a loud, muffled, conversation. I took a deep breath, smiled to myself, and went to work.

She came back a few minutes later, just as I was sopping up the last of the gravy with a thick slab of sourdough. She yanked away my plate and threw in a large slice of pie that wasn't on the menu either.

I looked up at her, waiting for some snappy remark about my eating habits, her favorite subject. Not this time.

"Here's the deal," she said quietly, shoving herself back into the booth.

"Isn't that my line?"

"No! You get one deal, one time, that's it."

"I don't think my client would like that very much. She can't pay but I kinda feel obliged to finish this, I'm the one found her."

"Don't worry about that," She carefully laid the note book down in front of me, opened it and pointed a pudgy finger at a series of letters and numbers on a page. "See this here, he's got a few connections, enough to see you straight so long as you keep your big yap shut."

"That's it?" I growled. "All I been through and all I get is sayonara, sucker?"

She took that remark with a straight face, although it stung like I'd just smacked her. "Word I get it was an accident, wasn't supposed to happen. And it won't happen again."

"That's comforting to know, but there's more to it, isn't there."

"I keep this," she said, "and you walk, period."

"Not good enough."

"What do you mean, not good enough! That's all the enough you're gonna get, so take it and run!"

There was a moment of silence while I thought it over. I didn't have all the details, but I figured I was close enough they would start coming my way. That seemed to be upsetting a lot of people, including her.

Stella took a deep breath, let it out hard and fast, and sat back in the booth. She stared at her pudgy palms while she spoke. "So, here's the thing. You gotta bunch of lonely old guys, real loaded, want a little company, maybe get married. Don't want nothin' local, don't want to make a big deal about it. Constantine shows up, says he can bring in a buncha dames from somewhere. Smart, good looking, won't ask too many questions, just looking to settle down, quiet like."

"Hide, you mean."

"Does it matter? They get married, get papers and a new name, a new life maybe, who knows." She sighed heavily.

"Except somewhere along the line it all goes south, right? Someone gets greedy maybe, ups the ante. Someone gets spooked and tries to bail?" I was leaning forward now, all but in her face, as the truth finally started to come out, along with all that sunlight called freedom. Mine.

"Something like that." She was still talking to her hands, afraid to face me over what I knew had to be the real secret to all this. She'd known the whole time and hadn't said a word. I didn't know whether to laugh or cry.

"And then I trip over her one night and stick my nose into it. Somebody doesn't like that and tries to put a stop to it, meanwhile I'm all over town trying to find her killer and not get killed myself."

"Like that's ever gonna happen." She looked up at me, square in the face. "You're too smart for that, or lucky. Either way I keep the book, certain parties have an interest in it. They get the book and anything else you might have and you walk away. Period."

"Just like that?"

"Just like that."

"And these certain parties?"

"Have been holding back a little. They know what you're like on a case, so they were sitting back, waiting for the right time. What happened to her was wrong but she had other connections to certain parties. They'll look after all of them, I promise."

So that was that, the puzzle wasn't finished, nor was it going to be. The rest of the pieces weren't coming out to play so the consolation prize was my walking away from it all. I didn't know how I felt about that but it seems I was going to have no choice in the matter. I didn't think Addy was going to be any happier with the outcome either, but sometimes you just take what you can get. I took a deep breath and exhaled hard.

"Okay, let's talk."